SHARK AND CHIPS AND O

With authors such as Anne Fine, Brough Girling, Bernard Ashley, Ann Pilling and Jill Paton Walsh, and favourite characters like Mr Browser, Super Gran and Vera Pratt, who could resist this terrific collection of stories, published together for the very first time?

There are hilarious stories such as Henry Hangs On and Shark and Chips, spooky stories like The Tin Telephone, family stories like William Darling, as well as modern and traditional folk-tales – in fact there's something for everyone to enjoy.

All the stories were originally published in *Puffin Post*, the magazine of the Puffin Book Club. For information about the Puffin Book Club, write to The Puffin Book Club Manager, Penguin Books, 27 Wrights Lane, London W8 5TZ.

Shark and Chips
and other stories

from the magazines
of the Puffin Book Club

PUFFIN BOOKS

PUFFIN BOOKS

Published by the Penguin Group
Penguin Books Ltd, 27 Wrights Lane, London W8 5TZ, England
Penguin Books USA Inc., 375 Hudson Street, New York, New York 10014, USA
Penguin Books Australia Ltd, Ringwood, Victoria, Australia
Penguin Books Canada Ltd, 10 Alcorn Avenue, Toronto, Ontario, Canada M4V 3B2
Penguin Books (NZ) Ltd, 182–190 Wairau Road, Auckland 10, New Zealand

Penguin Books Ltd, Registered Offices: Harmondsworth, Middlesex, England

First published 1992
1 3 5 7 9 10 8 6 4 2

The Acknowledgements on page 160 constitute an extension of this copyright page

Printed in England by Clays Ltd, St Ives plc
Set in Monophoto Baskerville

Contents

Shark and Chips

by K.M. Peyton
Illustrated by Tony Blundell

'**S**am's leaving at the end of term!'
Loopy, loony Sam, they couldn't believe
it. They were really fond of him.

'Why, sir?'

'It's all got too much for me. I can't seem
to manage any more.'

'You can manage us, sir!'

He looked doubtful, the stringy, eye-
blinking, nerve-ticking, well-meaning form
master of 4A.

'What are you going to do, sir?'

'I'm going to run a restaurant.'

They gaped. Sam, at the thought of the
blissful peace of running a restaurant after
running 4A, smiled happily. 'French food,'
he said dreamily.

'Sir, honestly!' Nutty MacTavish felt
insulted that he could prefer food to them.
All the same, she was sorry. 'I mean, he's all
right. We like him. What's he want to ditch
us for?' Nutty glared through her contact

lenses at her two friends, drippy Hoomey and the elegant Jaswant Singh. Nothing ever ruffled Jazz.

'He'll be happier with food,' he said amiably. 'Good luck to him, I say.'

'We ought to get him a present,' Hoomey said, thinking how low he must rate in old Sam's esteem. 'A leaving present.'

'No money!'

'We could do something.'

'Like what? Sing and dance?'

'Food,' said Jazz. 'Very appropriate. Take him out for a meal.'

'It costs a bomb!' Nutty scowled.

Jazz grinned. 'Make him one.'

'What, us?'

'I can't cook,' said Nutty.

'Anyone can cook. It's all in books,' Jazz said. 'You just read it up.'

It wasn't a bad idea at all. Nutty always made the decisions. She was a tank-like, bombastic, thirteen-year-old, a girl of wearisome energy and opinion. Hopeless Hoomey depended on her utterly, operating under her kindly wing, while Jazz liked her style and shared her lordly indifference to general opinion. He let her take the lead, unless it really mattered.

'You cook it then,' Nutty said.

'Women cook, not men.'

'Go on! All these Indian restaurants – not a woman to be seen!'

'Me, I Eengleesh,' said Jazz, grinning.
'Eengleeshmen no cook.'

Nutty hit him with a book, but he held
her wrists in an easy, steely grip. After some
argument they agreed a strategy: a course
each. Hoomey the starters, Nutty the main
course and Jazz the pudding. They would
invite Sam to Nutty's house the night her
parents went down the pub. Nutty's father
was a greengrocer.

'Sam's not a vegetarian,' Jazz said to her
firmly. 'Remember in France . . . that wild
boar he got steamed up about? You can't
just give him free spinach.'

Nutty looked disappointed.

'Meat,' Jazz said sternly.

'He seemed to like wine too,' Hoomey
remembered.

'Yes, all proper dinners have wine. You
can get the wine, Hoomey. Starters is the
cheapest course after all. A bottle of wine.'

Sam was enchanted with his invitation.

'What a kind thought! To do it all
yourselves too – I really appreciate that. It
will mean far more than just a present. I am
really looking forward to it.'

This worried Nutty slightly. 'We're not
really cooks, sir. But we're going to do our
best.'

'A fine spirit, Deirdre. You've always
shown initiative. I give you that.'

Nutty decided to show initiative in her main course. Not just sausages or lamb or something boring. The butcher didn't have wild boar, or even venison. Nutty explained her need.

'You can get shark in Galway,' the butcher said. Nutty worked out that Galway, being on the west coast of Ireland, was rather far to go shopping.

'My old aunty's coming over next week. I could get her to bring a few shark steaks. Would that suit you?'

'Yeah! That'd be great!'

Shark and chips, Nutty decided – that was real class. Not your old cod or plaice. The two boys were impressed. 'You'd better make your course as smart! I'm setting the standard.'

'Hope you know how to cook it,' Jazz said dubiously. 'Is it like a joint? Or fish?'

Nutty had no idea.

'It's a mammal,' Hoomey said, 'Like a whale.'

'Are you sure?'

Hoomey wasn't, but remained silent. It was more impressive. It put his idea of boring prawn cocktail in the shade. He looked through his mother's cookery books but she only had two: one for slimmers and one for people who lived in one room with only a gas ring. One of the slimming recipes said halve a cucumber lengthways and scoop out the pips, making a sort of boat. You put

things in the boat. This appealed to Hoomey
– his simple mind thinking boats rather went
with sharks – but the book wasn't very
specific in what you put in the boat. 'Dice
the flesh', it said, but this turned out to be
salmon, which Hoomey discovered was very
expensive.

When he asked Jazz, Jazz said, 'Whiskas,'
and laughed.

'Thanks for your help,' Hoomey said
sniffily.

'Man, there's nothing to starters. Put baked
beans in, or cornflakes, or Smarties. Use your
imagination. An eel would fit, wouldn't it?
How about an eel?'

Hoomey felt slightly queasy. 'Fish, you think?'

'Yeah, fish. If the shark's meat, that is.
Beats me how a shark can be meat but you
said it was.'

Eventually Hoomey found a tin of salmon
very cheap (a year past the Sell By date) and
decided to put that in, with a good lashing of
salad cream on top to cover any stale taste
there might be. Carried away with
excitement, he then put a row of cocktail
cherries along the top. He didn't say anything
about the Sell By date. The others were quite
impressed.

'Very pretty,' said Nutty. 'Are you sure
cocktail cherries go with salad cream?'

But Nutty was considering her four

enormous shark steaks from Galway with a
worried eye. She was absorbed with her own
problem. She didn't know whether to fry them
or put them in the oven.

'Put them in the oven,' Jazz advised. 'My
pud's got to go in the oven, so we can do 'em
together.'

'What's your pud?'

'Rhubarb crumble.'

'That's not very smart!' Nutty crowed.
'That's school dinner stuff. Thought you said
smart food?'

'It's going to have chocolate sauce on top,
instead of custard. That's the smart bit.
Pedigree cooking. You wait. Hot. I'm going
to hot it up just beforehand.'

He produced a saucepan full of congealed chocolate and put it on the stove.

'There, all ready to go.'

'You help me cut the chips then, and Hoomey can lay the table. You got the wine Hoomey?'

'Yes, I got two bottles,' Hoomey said proudly.

They had been in a To Clear bin at the local garage, two for the price of one.

'You can be host then, when he comes, while Jazz and I get on with the cooking.'

Too late, Nutty realized she had designed a dinner that needed total concentration just when the guest of honour arrived. She had to time the chips to be ready a few minutes after they finished Hoomey's yukky-looking starters. It was all going to be a bit fraught. Even unflappable Jazz was worried about how long his rhubarb crumble would take and kept switching it from shelf to shelf in the oven.

'Shut the door, or my sharks'll never be cooked in time!' Nutty wailed.

'You want to get the fat heating for the chips,' Jazz said, 'Or they'll be soggy.'

'I know how to cook chips!'

Chips for four seemed to be rather a lot for the chip-pan but Nutty jammed them all in, just in time to greet old Sam as Hoomey ushered him into the kitchen. He looked all round, beaming his kindly smile.

'This looks very nice! I'm really going to enjoy this! Give me a few ideas for my restaurant, eh?'

'It's pretty lush, sir. Irish shark steaks,' Jazz said modestly.

Nutty shot him a hard look, for stealing her thunder.

'I ordered them specially from Galway,' she said firmly, treading on Jazz's foot. He was worried about his chocolate sauce, fixed like concrete in the pan.

'I'll just put this on very low,' he said.

Everything seemed to be under control, so Nutty took her apron off and sat down at the table. Jazz pulled out the best chair for Sam, and poured the wine. They talked about cooking and Nutty and Jazz made out they were dab hands at tossing up an impressive dinner, while Hoomey decided that, no, cocktail cherries didn't go with salad cream. The salmon underneath tasted very peculiar, but no one mentioned it. Only he knew about the Sell By date so he supposed it was all in the mind. Everyone ate it, although not with any great display of relish.

By the time they had finished strange smells were coming from the oven, and Jazz discovered that the chip-pan was splashing a lot of fat into his chocolate sauce. He moved it over, hoping no one would notice. Nutty opened the oven and gave a wail.

'What's up?'

The rhubarb crumble had bubbled over and the shark steaks were covered with a layer of rhubarb. As they peered into the

oven, heads together, it occurred to both of
them simultaneously that this was a disaster
that needed to be covered up.

'Turn them over,' Jazz hissed.

He snatched the fish-slice from the drawer
and kicked Hoomey in passing to make him
keep Sam in polite conversation. While he
scraped the shark steaks into new positions,
rhubarb side down, Nutty was discovering
that yes, the chip-pan was too small to cook
so many chips. They were soft and dispirited,
bubbling wetly in a big sorry mass. She lifted
them out. There was nothing to be done
about it. The shark was already burned and
not to be left with Jazz's lethal pudding
another minute longer. She put the chips into
their dish, trying to shake them apart,
without success. They were a funny grey
colour. The shark steaks looked peculiar too,
and smelled more so, of burned sugar.

'Have some more wine,' she suggested
brightly to Sam. If he drank enough he
wouldn't notice. She dished up grimly.

Sam's heroic smile did not falter.

'My word, very original! Not too much
Deirdre – the starter was very filling, and
there's a pudding to come.'

Even Nutty was hard put to it to eat her
shark steak and chips, and keep up a cheerful
conversation. But she had to prove it was
edible. Sam did his best, but his smile became
glazed, and beads of sweat stood out on his

forehead. Hoomey kept his head down, chewing manfully, and panicking at the thought of throwing up, while Jazz eventually pushed his steak and chips to one side and left the table with his plate 'to see to my pudding'. A clever move, the others recognized enviously.

He brought out the rhubarb crumble. The rhubarb having burst through the crumble, the top looked like a dark-brown varnish. The chocolate sauce was bubbling merrily, well stuck to the bottom of the pan, and with big grease blobs from the chip-pan dimpling the surface. Jazz poured it into a jug and stirred the fat in, and brought the pudding to the table. Nutty collected the shark plates, wanly scraping the limp chips into the bin, recognizing disaster when it stared her in the face.

'Rhubarb crumble and chocolate sauce!' Sam croaked, trying to look cheerful. 'Just a very small portion for me.'

Even Jazz was a paler shade of brown. He had to get a knife to penetrate the 'crumble', and would have done better with a hammer and chisel.

'Sorry it's a bit well done,' he mumbled.

Sam laughed nervously. 'I'm sure it's delicious.'

That's why they liked him: he was such an optimist, always believing the best of them. They were terribly sorry it hadn't worked out. They watched him depart from the front door. He staggered down the path and stopped, bending over the straggly privet hedge by the gate.

'What's he doing?' Hoomey asked, peering into the darkness.

'He's throwing up,' Nutty said sadly.

'Better not let him think we know. He'll be embarrassed.' Jazz shut the door very quietly.

'I think I'm going to throw up too,' he added.

'And me.'

'And me.'

They all ran.

The Fancy-dress Party

by Marjorie Darke

Have you ever noticed how the really big
happenings in people's lives nearly always
start with something so small it's ridiculous?
I'm talking about things like catching a bus,
spur of the moment. Not any old bus, mind
you, but the one carrying a stranger who
becomes your best mate. Or casually picking
up a book on juggling and ending up a circus
star. Or even something as trivial as asking a
question . . .

About nine months ago *I* asked a question,
and the thought of it still gnaws at me. Zoe
and Wesley keep telling me not to be daft;
that no one in their right mind would ever
blame me for what happened. I wish I could
believe them. But it wasn't only the question,
it was *who* I asked. I ought to have known
better because they were mates of mine. We'd

been all through Juniors and Comprehensive together. So you see, I knew them very well: Silas and Tom – Brains and Beef. Complete opposites. Silas looks like a pea-stick topped by a mop while Tom is the barn-door type, but in spite of all the differences they didn't entirely hate each other's guts. In fact they went around together with the rest of us. But they had always been rivals. Put them together, add my question *and* the fact that they both fancied Zoe – result: DYNAMITE!

Judge for yourselves.

We had been loafing around the town centre most of that chilly December morning. It was Saturday – about the only time we did all get together since Wesley and Tom had become part of the Great Unwaged after the end of the summer term. Zoe and I had gone back to school in September for exam retakes. Silas had gone back too, but as he'd scooped A-grades in nearly everything, he was now one of the proper sixth-form gods. Which made it all the more unlikely he would continue to bother with us. But he did.

'To show off,' Tom said.

'Don't be so hard on him! He's always gone around with us,' Zoe said. 'Just because he's brainy doesn't mean he hasn't any feelings.' Which was a sideways dig at Tom who isn't known for his academic brilliance, though his skills on the rugger field have to be seen to be believed.

But to get back to this particular Saturday and my question . . .

We'd finally wandered into Market Square. I'd just finished my last bag of crisps, and we were all skint. There didn't seem to be anything to do and boredom was settling in, but for some reason we went on hanging about. No one seemed to want to be the first to push off home. It was at this point I threw out the fateful question.

'Do you believe in ghosts?'

'You kidding?' Wesley grinned broadly. 'That old nonsense!'

'Load of rubbish,' Tom agreed.

Silas suddenly rounded on them both. 'You can't make statements like that without facts. All you're doing is chucking half-baked prejudices about . . .'

'You mean you *do* believe in ghosts?' I butted in, astonished.

'As usual you jump in with both feet, Anna,' he said. 'Before you interrupted I had been going to point out that to be correctly scientific, concrete evidence must be produced first – relevant material for or against the subject under review. Otherwise it's impossible to draw objective, worthwhile conclusions. And without this system any beliefs are highly suspect. So you can't . . .'

'Oh shut it, man!' Wesley gave me a pained look. 'What did you have to ask a fool question like that for, Anna? You know

what he's like. Might just as well stuff 50p
into a talking machine – you reckoning to be
a teacher, Silas, old buddy?'

'No,' Silas said. 'I intend going on to
university to read biochemistry with a view
to winning a research fellowship.'

The rest of us burst into a groan of laughter,
which went on for longer than necessary
because we all knew it was on the cards he
would do exactly what he said. Silas was
relentless when he set his mind on something.

Of course I know now I should have let
things drift, but some little devil urged me on
to give another stir. I looked at Tom and
Wesley. 'He's got a point. How come you
two are so convinced? For all you know there
might be an eight-foot ghost right here.' I
pointed towards the giant plastic ice-cream
cone outside the supermarket. 'Can't you see
it? A weird hooded figure with horrible
glowing eyeballs and fangs dripping blood.
Just because you aren't turned into ghosties
doesn't mean they don't exist.' My
imagination has always been sharp, so my
shudder wasn't all acting.

'You can't count,' Wesley said. 'There are
two. Polish your specs, Anna, and take
another butchers. See in that third trolley
along, with the bow-ties and rabbit ears?
Crouching ready to spring they are. Two
white see-through spoo . . . ooo . . . ooooks!'
and he began to drift around flapping his

arms and moaning eerily to himself.

'Hardly fair,' Zoe said, serious now. 'Silas wants facts and all you do is kid on about one or two, tall-short hooded-eared ghosts. Anyone with half an eye and the merest touch of ESP knows there are three of them sitting on the bench, and they're *green*!'

Silas, who brightened when she began, now realized she was taking the micky. His normally pale face flamed, and I felt almost sorry for him, until Tom asked: 'What's ESP?'

It was a dumb question but Silas needn't have been so cutting.

'Extra sensory perception, clown. Something you couldn't possibly have.' He was *withering*. Without another word to any of us, he swung away and loped along the pavement to the corner, turned and disappeared from sight.

The friendliness of the morning clouded over with him pushing off in a huff. There didn't seem much point in standing about in the cold. We drifted back to our various homes.

Somehow from then on the Saturday meetings dwindled. Wesley got a job, and soon after, he and Zoe (who was leaving school at the end of term) started going out together. I was up to my neck in school work and the Christmas Review. Our ways parted. Occasionally I'd see Tom in the distance. At school, Silas and I would nod in passing, but

that was all. Though once, when I went to
the public library in search of stuff for a
history project, I came across him bent over
a crabby little book. He was miles away.

On impulse I tapped him on the shoulder.
'Hi!'

He nearly hit the roof. 'Oh . . . hallo,
Anna.' He pulled himself together with an
effort. 'What are you doing here?'

I was slightly irritated. He had this knack
of hinting you were a goof with not too much
between the ears. Probably didn't mean it,
but I wanted to shake him a bit. 'Looking
for info on Tudor church architecture – tomb
sculpture mainly.' I was pleased to see his
surprise. 'What's that you're reading?'

His arm slid across the book. 'Like you – a
bit of research. The atomic structure of blood
cells. Very dry stuff!' and he laughed.

I hadn't got my reading specs on at the
time, but that book didn't look up-to-date
enough to be anything to do with atoms. I
couldn't imagine why he wanted to be so
secretive, but after all it wasn't any business
of mine. I forgot all about him and his book
with the pressure of getting my project
finished before the end of term, plus the frenzy
of last rehearsals which kept going wrong.

Of course the Review was all right on the
night. After a fifth curtain call, Zoe and Wes
came backstage and found me.

'You cagey old devil!' Zoe gave me a hug. 'You never let on you could sing like that.'

'And act. Fantastic!' Wes patted me on the back. 'We should go out and celebrate. What d'you say?'

'We're having a party now, backstage. Just cast and stage-hands, I'm afraid. Sorry,' and I truly meant it.

'Tomorrow then,' Zoe suggested.

Tomorrow was the first day of the holidays. 'We're off to my gran's. We always go for Christmas.'

'Never mind. Tell you what, we can double up with Tom's birthday party.' She rooted in her shoulder-bag. 'Almost forgot – he asked me to give you this,' handing me a large grey envelope.

The card inside had a picture of a black-hooded figure with silver fangs and drops of red blood plopping down each side. Sitting on a bench at the bottom were what looked like three green sheets holding up a banner which said 'GHOST PARTY' in dripping red letters. The other side of the card invited me to come to Tom's house, eight o'clock on New Year's Eve in 'Fancy Ghost Dress'.

'Tom'll be OK,' Wes said solemnly. He'll only need a fan.'

Zoe and I stared at him.

'For fancy dress,' he explained. 'Tom fan,' and when we stayed blank; '*Phantom*, you jelly-heads!'

I pasted his cheek with some of my make-up removal cold cream for that.

I went as a shadow to Tom's party. The costume was dead easy. I'd already got a black leotard, tights and gloves. All I had to make was a sort of balaclava out of black paper with slits for my eyes.

Tom lived just beyond the church in what used to be an old stone farmhouse before the estate grew up round it and swallowed all the fields. But there was still a biggish garden full of spooky trees. He opened the door to me. No mistaking him in spite of the doggie-mask he was wearing – his square shape gave him away, and the rugger kit.

'Who are you?' Tom asked.

I lifted my balaclava. 'More to the point, who are *you*? What sort of a ghost has a dog's head?'

'Hi, Anna!' He thumped his chest. 'I'm a Familiar Spirit. Like witches have – cats and dogs and all that.'

'Don't get too familiar with me!'

'You'll be lucky!' he grinned and stood back. 'Come on in. The others are here.'

By 'the others' I took it he meant our old gang, but there was quite a mob I either didn't know at all, or knew vaguely as rugger friends of Tom's – though it wasn't easy to see much. The spookiness had crept inside. A few dim candle lanterns hung from the ceiling, black and silver streamers floated everywhere, and several of those plastic skeletons dangled on the walls. The only unspooky thing was the music bursting through the house. I glimpsed Wes and Zoe dancing in the main room. Nearer, lounging against the open door was a tall spindly figure in an old grey dressing-gown. Silas! I mentally chalked up one to Tom for being big-hearted enough to invite him, though as the evening wore on I began to think differently. It was plain that Silas was no party man, in sharp contrast to Tom who was the life and soul. I decided it was a cunning way of getting his own back, especially in front of Zoe.

Silas turned, and I saw that he had a woolly toy perched on his shoulder – a chewed-looking black cat with a white tail that had a black tip. He hadn't pinned it on very well and the thing kept slipping. He looked a right freak.

I went over. 'Don't tell me – that's another Familiar Spirit,' pointing at the moggie, 'and you're a wizard.'

'Short on observation as usual, Anna,' he said. 'Look!' He held out an old leather bag containing a bottle of cider and a small cage with a mouse in it.

'So . . . wizards drink cider and keep mice – what's new?'

'I'm an alchemist,' he said shortly.

I must have looked blank.

'A medieval chemist,' he explained. 'Mostly

they spent their time either trying to turn base metal into gold, or they experimented with potions that would keep you alive for ever. Now d'you understand?' He hitched the woolly toy back on to his shoulder, but it refused to settle, and he gave it another impatient tug. 'Stay *there*, Maxie.'

It seemed a feeble fancy dress to me. 'Where's the ghost connection?'

'What people think of as being ghostly is usually nothing but a demonstration of personal ignorance. When they can't come up with a logical reason, they indulge in supernatural make-believe – ghosts or magic or some other twaddle.' He always had this heavy way of talking, but now he seemed almost aggressive.

'Silas,' I said, 'this is a *party*, remember?'

He frowned. 'I'm not a complete idiot. If you can be patient long enough you'll see I've prepared a special party trick.' He felt for the open leather bag, fingers gripping the bottle-neck. I saw his knuckles shine white. I also saw the little snout twitching between the bars of the cage. An uneasy feeling crept over me.

'You aren't going to hurt that mouse are you? I can't stand it when people muck about with animals.'

'Don't be ridiculous!' He let go of the bottle, putting his hand on my shoulder – to reassure me I suppose, but it did the opposite. I could feel him tremble. Anxiety seemed to flow from

him and infect me, which made it all the
worse. His face had a greenish look. I began
to feel slightly sick and shivery, and very cold.
There was a musty smell in my nose.

'Are you two all right?' Zoe was gazing at
us. 'You look awful.'

I swallowed hard. 'Yes.' I didn't want
questions. 'It's nothing . . . someone just
walked over my grave, that's all.' The silly
phrase seemed to work, because she giggled
and said: 'Well it is a ghost party!'

After that I slid away from Silas and joined
the dancing to warm myself up and to try
and shake off the remains of the anxious
feeling which still hung around.

Near midnight, one of Tom's rugger mates
switched off the record-player and shouted
'Belt up all of you. Move yourselves . . .
GANGWAY! Let the man through!'

We shuffled closer together as Tom came in
from the kitchen carrying one of those old-
fashioned, round, iron pots. The sort people
used to hang on a hook over an open fire. In
front of the window was a table with a large
cork mat, a mass of mugs and two plates piled
with cut-up birthday cake. Tom set the pot
down on the mat, said: 'Hang about!' and
disappeared to the kitchen again, coming back
waving a ladle. Silas was hunched against the
wall deliberately refusing to be interested. As
Tom brushed by, I saw him reach into Silas's
bag and nick the bottle. It was a really clever

bit of thieving. Silas never felt a thing.

'Drinking time!' Tom announced. 'Mum's special Witch-brew. To go with the cake and the New Year.'

There was a cheer. Somebody called: 'What's in it, Tom?' and got answering shouts like: 'Frogs' and 'Worm gut' amongst other nasties. Somebody else yelled: 'Any booze, that's what I want to know?'

'There will be,' Tom held up a cider bottle. 'Contribution from old Silas there! Thanks mate – just the thing to give it extra kick!' and he started to unscrew the top.

Behind me there was a sudden commotion, then Silas saying urgently: 'Don't, Tom!' as he pushed past.

But Tom either didn't hear, or chose not to. He had removed the cap and started to tip the bottle.

'NO!' roared Silas, launching himself across the table, snatching at the bottle, missing and hitting Tom's arm instead. Green liquid spurted from the bottle-neck over both of them, some of it splashing down into the gently steaming pot. It reacted by sending up a great belch of cloudy fog that spread into the room. Before it became too dense and overpowering, I saw two shapes – they could only have been Silas and Tom – arch away from each other, then curl up and contort as if some outside energy was forcing, crushing their bodies into ever smaller more grotesque

positions. My eyes started to stream as if I
had been peeling onions. My throat burned.
Imagine how it feels to run through stinging
nettles, and you will have some idea of the
state of my skin – an all-over itching fiery
mass. Tears were blinding me. Everyone was
coughing. Some people made a great
blundering rush for the door in an attempt
to get out. Elbowing, shoving, getting stuck
and swearing. Believe me, panic is catching!
Soon we were all fighting and battering our
way out of the house into the pitch dark garden.

The icy air cooled us down pretty fast,
though someone went on having hysterics.
The rest of us began to get a grip of ourselves.
Mopping my streaming eyes, I saw Wes and
Zoe huddled together at the bottom of the
steps. I went over to them. The front door
was wide open. A shaft of brighter light came
from the party room.

'What the hell happened?' Wesley was
rubbing his face with the back of his hand.

Couldn't . . . see.' Zoe's teeth were
chattering. 'Anyone . . . hurt?'

I tried not to think about what I'd seen.
'Dunno.'

'Oughtn't we to find out?' Wes was looking
at me.

'Go back in *there* you mean?'

'Well we can't just stand here. Where are
Tom and Silas? *Someone*'ll have to go and look.'

He was right, of course. Reluctantly we

screwed up what was left of our courage and went indoors.

The room had that after-the-party look. Chairs shoved anyhow. Plates with half-eaten sausages on broken sticks. Bits of curling sandwiches. Crumbs and squashed cheese walked into the carpet. The iron pot was still on the table but it wasn't round any more. It looked as if someone had shoved it into a furnace. The rim was all buckled and what looked like a stream of molten metal had trickled down one side on to the cork mat, eating a hole right through to the table. A sickly acid smell hung in the air − burned fat and rotting vegetables is the only way I can describe it.

Nobody was there. Nobody at all.

That was the end of the party. It might well have been the end of the affair, if Tom and Silas had turned up. When they didn't there was the most monumental fuss − demented parents, police, journalists making a meal of us. You can imagine, it was very upsetting. Not something I'd want to go through again. Bad enough if they'd been two kids from school I'd only known vaguely, but Tom and Silas had been my friends for years. Gradually though, things quietened. THE END you might think . . . But not quite.

February arrived. On a raw day with a nipping wind and some pale sun that blinked round the clouds every now and again, I

went up to the church with my camera and
Zoe. The aim was to take a photograph of
the Blake Family Tomb. They'd been local
Lords of the Manor until they'd run out of
heirs and the name died out. A few
photographs would fill out my history project.
You see, what with Christmas Review, then
all the havoc, I'd left it only three-quarters
done. Zoe came along because she hadn't
anything particular to do that day.

I'd got permission to take photographs
inside the church, and took the first picture
but wasn't quite satisfied. I was just about to
take a second when Zoe let out a squeak.
She was standing pressed against the end of a
pew, kicking at a small moth-eaten cat that
was trying to rub round her ankles.

'Get off . . . *get off*! Anna do something
can't you?'

I'd never realized before that she didn't
like cats. I said: 'It's only a kitten,' going to
pick it up, but the thing leaped away from
me and bolted into a dark corner.

My neck-hairs prickled, and the feeling
travelled down my spine.

A black cat *with a white tail tipped with black*.

I found it rubbing along the wall just below
one of those In-Memory-Of tablets. I
managed to grab the kitten and just as I did,
the sun blinked again sending a shaft of light
on the tablet. The letters were very worn but
still legible.

Here lie the Mortall Remaynes of
Brother Silvius
Cutt Downe in the Flowere of Yewthe
Anno Domini 1313
Lord Have Mercie

There was a carving underneath. A figure in relief wearing a monk's robe, hands tucked into sleeves.

I looked at the monk's face, and felt as if I'd been punched in the stomach.

'Silas!' I must have gasped his name out loud because Zoe said: 'What?' and came over to see.

I pointed, and we both stood there gaping like thickies. The kitten started to wriggle. I must have been clutching it rather tightly, but now I dropped it as if it were red-hot. It made a bee-line for Zoe who let out another screech and fled, kitten racing at her heels.

I had enough sense left to use my camera a second time before nerves got the upper hand and I pelted after them into the fresh air. They were almost at the bottom of the hill and I was half-way down when the dog started yapping.

You may well ask, what dog? I'd never seen one like it around here before. I didn't see much now, it was going too fast. Whisking past me – a flash of stocky body on short powerful legs. I began to run and saw it catch up with Zoe, but the little cat was too cunning. It sprang – a small, black arch of electric hair, extended claws and open, spitting mouth. The dog skidded to a halt, but too late for escape. A small, deadly paw struck. The dog recoiled with yelps and snapping snarls. Zoe jumped back – petrified, I could see. Then she bolted away from the hissing growling fight.

I couldn't take any more. I'd had enough for one day. Doubling back, I went the long way home. But when the photographs were developed I took them round to Zoe's house.

'The tomb has printed well, but the tablet is a rub-out.' What the sun hadn't over-exposed, I'd finished off with camera-shake. 'It doesn't prove anything, that's what's so maddening.'

Zoe didn't take this up, but sat biting her nails. Finally she burst out: 'What *am* I going to do? I can't get rid of either of them.'

I knew she meant the animals sitting outside her house. They'd been there when I arrived. Dog on step. Cat arched on fence. Getting indoors without them had been a skill.

'RSPCA?' I suggested.

'Doesn't seem right.'

I was glad she thought that way. It wouldn't have seemed right to me either. 'What does Wes have to say?'

'A mouthful! Last time he came round Tom bit him . . .' she slapped her hand across her mouth, eyes staring out at me over the top.

'Don't worry. I know they are Tom and Silas.'

'Don't worry?' She flared up. 'It isn't a
joke you know. They won't leave me alone.
And their eyes. Pleading . . .'

'All right, all right! They're trapped and we
should be doing something to get them back
to normal. But how?' I was just as upset as Zoe.

We looked at each other. Helpless.

That was three months ago. Nine since I asked
that first thoughtless question: 'Do you believe
in ghosts?'

Nine months ago I would have answered:
'No.' Now I'm not so sure.

Sometimes I go for a walk through the
churchyard and down to Tom's house
because I know he likes this. Oh . . . didn't
I tell you? Tom has taken to staying with me
now. He has an old mat by the fire in our
kitchen. He's good company, but I never look
directly into his eyes. I can't stand the silent
beseeching question I see there.

I've tried everything I can think of. I've
even tried to discover the name of that crabby
old library book Silas was reading. If only I
could ask him to tell me. But cats can't talk.
Not that I see him often. He doesn't haunt
Zoe so much these days. But now and again
on our walks he will materialize, apparently
from nowhere, and stand out of reach,
watching Tom and me as we pass by.

Super Gran's Pedal Power

by **Forrest Wilson**
Illustrated by David McKee

As Super Gran and company stepped off
the plane at Muglas, on the Isle of Gran,
they were greeted by Mr Hood, the island's
Sports Manager.

'It was good of you to come across from
the mainland to present the prizes for the
Pinta People's Pedal-Power Cycle Race.'

'Och, don't mention it, laddie. I've always
wanted to visit the Isle of Gran.'

He drove them from the airport into town
and along the promenade which overlooked
a long stretch of golden sand.

'Look at that,' Willard said, 'I fancy
having a go on that.'

He pointed to a four-wheeled beach-bike
that was making its leisurely way along the
prom. It was the sort of tandem which carried
two riders, each with a set of pedals, sitting
side-by-side on a seat.

Mr Hood drove the car up a side street and into a busy town square, full of shops, where a temporary wooden platform had been erected.

'Well here we are, folks. The race starts, and finishes, here each day.'

'Each day?' exclaimed Edison. 'Is it on for more than one day?'

'Yes, it's a six-day race,' he explained. 'The cyclists do six stages altogether, one stage each day. And each stage winner receives the yellow jersey, which he wears the next day. Points are awarded to the leading contestants on each stage and whoever wins the most points is the overall winner and wins the trophy.'

'Just like the Tour de France,' Willard added.

'So could you be here at three o'clock, Super Gran, to start the final stage of the race? And then return about an hour later, to present the prizes to the winners?'

'Aye, sure laddie, nae bother at a',' she assured him, with a grin, then translated it into English. 'It's no bother at all. It'll be easy-peasy.'

'I'll see you later. And thanks again.' He drove off, to return to his office.

'This race sounds like the ones on the Isle of Man,' Willard informed them. 'The TT motor-cycle races.'

'But this is the Isle of *Gran* and this is the Pinta People's cycle races,' Edison reminded him. 'So it's not so much the "tea-tea" races, it's more the "milk-milk" races!' she laughed.

'Let's go back to the prom,' Willard

suggested. 'I want to have a go on those beach-bike things.'

'Good idea, Willie,' Super Gran agreed. 'We'll have a wee shot at them while we're waiting for the race to start. It'll be ages yet.'

'But are you sure we've got time?' Edison asked. 'Mr Hood said to be back at three o'clock.'

'Havers, lassie, we've got loads of time,' Super Gran assured her, glancing at her watch. 'It's only half-past one.'

Willard eagerly led the way to the shop on the prom which hired out the machines and after they'd paid their money he and Super Gran jumped on to the seat and put their feet on their individual pedals.

'There's not enough room for three people, lassie,' Super Gran said, 'but there's a wee seat behind us. You don't mind sitting there facing backwards, do you?'

'Oh, I'm not bothered about having a ride,' Edison assured her.

'Of course you are, lassie,' Super Gran insisted. 'Just climb on to that wee bit o' seat. You'll be safe there.'

Edison started to argue, but Willard put a stop to that!

'Hurry up if you're coming! Our time'll be up before you get on.'

'I still don't think we've got time for this,' she persisted as she clambered aboard and they set off.

They cycled along the prom and back into the town square.

'See,' Super Gran said as they slowly pedalled their way through it, 'the cyclists haven't arrived yet. We've got loads of time. I told you.'

'Gran, let's go the way the race goes,' Willard suggested.

'Aye, good idea, Willie,' she agreed.

So they made their way through the streets of Muglas, following the red markers attached to the shops, houses and walls which indicated the race route.

Presently it led them out of town and along leafy lanes and hilly country roads which wound their way up, down and around the island, letting them view the Isle of Gran from every conceivable angle.

'Look, there's the coast down there,' said Edison, pointing back towards it. 'And I can see a little train chugging its way up the mountain railway, and the . . .'

'Never mind the train chugging up the mountain,' Willard snorted. 'What about me and Gran chugging our way up *this* mountain!'

Pedalling was too much like hard work.

It had been bad enough doing it on the level, on the streets of Muglas, and having to haul Edison around as a passenger, but it was really hard going trying to do it on the steep hills.

'It's your turn to do a bit of pedalling,' he moaned at her.

'Och, I'll do it for the two of us,' Super Gran offered. 'You just put your feet up and have a rest and I'll do the pedalling.'

'No, I'll take a turn,' Edison said, 'you'll strain yourself.'

But then she suddenly yelled: 'Hey! Look out!' and pointed excitedly.

'What is it?' Super Gran glanced over her shoulder to see what was wrong. 'Jings!'

Edison was pointing at a swarm of cyclists who had appeared, from nowhere, over the crest of a hill behind them and who, crouched low over their handlebars, were just about to descend on them – at what seemed like one hundred miles an hour!

'Gerrout-the-way, ya old crow!' the leader yelled as they went zooming past.

The draught from the scores of cycles caused the beach-bike to zig-zag crazily all over the narrow road.

'Hey! Mind out!' exclaimed Super Gran, 'you'll have us in the ditch!'

'Serves you right!' the leader shouted back at her.

'Hey, Gran!' Willard yelled, 'that's the race . . . !

'The race *you* were supposed to start!' Edison added. 'They started without you!'

'Aye,' she agreed, 'and I'm supposed to be there at the finish, to present the prizes.'

By now the last of the cyclists had whizzed past them and the country road was quiet again.

'They must've started early,' Willard said.

'What time is it?' Edison asked.

Super Gran glanced at her watch. 'It's only half-past one. Jings, that's funny, it was half-past one the last time I looked. Oh-oh,' – she shook it – 'it's stopped!'

'Oh, we're late!' Edison cried. 'We'll never catch up with them!'

'Who won't? Just watch this!' the old lady retorted, pressing down hard on the pedals.

'You'll never do it!'

Edison was aghast at the very idea, but Super Gran had the light of battle in her eye!

'The cheek o' yon wee bachles! Trying to knock us into the ditch! I'll show 'em!'

'Super Gran! What're you doing?' Edison gasped, seeing the old lady's feet spinning round at Super-speed, pedalling furiously to move the heavy, over-laden machine in pursuit of the racing cyclists, who by now were two or three miles ahead of them.

Super Gran glanced at Willard, and

warned him 'Keep your feet away from your
pedals – or they'll get knocked off!'

'And he'll be foot-loose!' Edison giggled.

Willard looked down at the Super-spinning
pedals, fearfully, and gulped. He could
imagine what would happen if his feet went
anywhere near them while his Gran was
Super-pedalling. It didn't bear thinking about!

'But you'll . . . never catch up . . . with
them,' gasped Edison, breathlessly, the speed
of the wind catching her breath.

'Who won't? Just watch me, lassie!' Super
Gran replied, as she pedalled even faster!

Edison clutched the side of her seat in
terror as the machine flew along the road
and caught up with the race's tail-enders.

'Huh? Yeeks! What the . . . ?' they gasped as
they were overtaken by a little old lady and
two spotty kids on an old, heavy, rusted
beach-bike going like the proverbial clappers!

Super Gran pinged the bell on the
handlebar, to clear the way through the
bunch. And she got some of her own back by
making *them* wobble, zig-zag and about to
fall into the ditch at the side of the road.

Then gradually she made her way, metre
by metre, through the mass of muscle-
rippling, sweaty cyclists until she squeezed the
beach-bike – with a little help from its
battered bicycle bell! – in amongst the race
leaders. And the leaders couldn't believe their

eyes when they saw who – and what – was joining them.

'Huh? Yeeks! What the . . .?' they gasped, echoing what the tail-enders had said a few minutes earlier.

Then suddenly, they were entering Muglas, where a crowd of cheering sightseers welcomed them. They passed the harbour and ran along the promenade before turning up towards the town square, where Super Gran managed to put on a last-minute spurt to pull herself ahead of the leaders. And she did it, to the deafening cheers of the crowds lining the square. She won the race!

And she actually *had* won this stage of the race, as she had faithfully followed the complete course of the race, from start to finish, even if she did have a start on the others! But, not realizing this, Mr Hood climbed on to the platform, a yellow jersey in his hand, and joined the two winning cyclists who were already there.

'Super Gran,' he announced, 'will now present the jersey to Cy Clist, the winner of the last stage of the Pinta People's Pedal-Power Six-Day Cycle Race.'

As the crowd applauded, Super Gran jumped off the beach-bike and leaped on to the platform.

'I have great pleasure,' she said, 'in presenting the jersey to the winner, the *real* winner, of the last stage of the race – me, Super Gran!'

And she took it from a shocked Mr Hood
and put it on herself, pulling it down over
her tartan tammy, on top of her cardigan.
Then she turned to Cy Clist, and added: 'The
old crow!' Cy blushed with embarrassment
and Edison, in the crowd, shouted up at him:
'Who's "crowing" now, eh? Ha, ha, ha!'

The crowd continued to cheer but all the
cyclists looked humiliated. Imagine being
beaten in a race by a little old lady, they
thought. And imagine her claiming the yellow
jersey, too.

But then she grinned, relented, pulled it off
again and presented it to Cy, which brought
a smile to his face and to the faces of his
glum chums.

'I was only joking, son,' she explained, a
twinkle in her eye. 'I couldn't resist it. Here
you are, you're the fastest cyclist in today's
race.' Then added: 'Apart from me, that is!'

Mr Hood, recovering from the shock,
whispered to her that she now had to award
the trophy to the man who had won the most
points during the six days.

'And that person,' he announced, 'is
Speedy Pedlar.'

As Speedy stepped forward Super Gran,
glancing at the crowd, spotted a group of
women assistants who had emerged from a
nearby shop, to watch the prize giving.

Suddenly, to everyone's amazement, she
leaped from the platform, ran to one of them

and spoke to her. At first the woman looked
puzzled, but then she took off her scarlet shop
overall and gave it to Super Gran who leaped
back on to the platform and presented it to
Speedy Pedlar.

'Here you are, son,' she said, 'this is for you!'

He blushed as scarlet as the scarlet garment
and stared at it.

'Huh? But what do I want with this?'

'It's an overall – and you're the "overall"
winner! Ha, ha, ha!' she laughed.

Everyone joined in, then Edison, with a
pretended pout, added: 'Hey, Super Gran,
that's not fair, that's the kind of joke that *I*
usually crack!'

Edison didn't get to crack the joke but, as
usual did have the last word!

Crash Landing

by **Gillian Cross**
Illustrated by Bob Harvey

. . . the helicopter soared upwards, as though someone had flicked it up and thrown it . . . Then it whirled away to the west and disappeared in the far distance . . .

Charity leaned back on her pillow. Three pages left. She'd have time to finish her book and find out what happened to the Demon Headmaster before Dad got in from his evening walk round the farmyard.

As she flipped the last page, there was a noise overhead, low in the sky. An engine coughed, stuttered. Louder – very loud – something scraped the roof, clanged in the gutter and swooshed past her window, huge and dark.

Then the light went out.

For a second it felt like the end of the world. Then the pigs began to squeal, chickens, squawked, goats bleated and the bull bellowed from his field beyond the sheep pasture.

Charity pushed her feet into her old trainers, threw the book down and leaped downstairs. Mum and Dad were outside with a big flashlight.

'Hey, wait!' Charity called across the yard.

Beyond them, in the light, she could see a tangled mess of telephone wires and electric cables twisted into the rotor of a helicopter. Below, jagged and glinting in the torchlight, was the broken glass bubble with a tall figure stiff and upright inside.

As she shouted, Dad turned and shone the light into her eyes, blinding her to everything else. 'Get inside, Charity!'

'But I want to help!'

'Fetch Tom then,' shouted Mum. 'He'll have to take the van and go to a phone-box.'

'But I don't – ' Charity started. Then realized that she didn't need details. They wanted everything. Fire, police and ambulance.

She raced along the footpath to Tom's cottage, sure-footed even in the dark. Past the broken gate that was held together with a loop of string, over the poached mud in the cow pasture, through the hole in the hedge where sheep escaped. Calling all the time.

'Tom! There's been an accident! The phone's dead. *Tom!*'

Suddenly he was there, appearing quietly as he always did, with his old cap pulled forward on his bald head. 'I'll take the van then. Never fear.'

That was all. No fuss. No questions. He put his arm round Charity's shoulder and they walked back. As they passed the tumbledown pigsty and came into the farmyard, Charity looked across at the helicopter. The tall, upright figure was still in the cockpit. Something about it made her shudder. Tom patted her arm.

'Off to bed now. No place for you.'

Charity stopped at the kitchen door and heard peace return as Tom walked into the farmyard. Squeals and squawks died away, replaced by occasional sleepy snuffles and clucks. And the sound of people talking.

It's all right, Charity thought, climbing the stairs. *Now Tom's come. He'll keep it all all right.*

The next thing she knew was waking up with the sunlight hot across her face and the sound of Alice, her pet lamb, baaing at the kitchen door. She sat up and looked at her watch.

Eleven o'clock? Jumping up, she pulled on her clothes and scurried down to the kitchen, calling out as she went. 'Why didn't you wake me up?'

Her mother was standing at the kitchen table, spreading a neat little lacy cloth on the best black tray. 'Sssh!'

'What?' Charity stopped at the bottom of the stairs.

'I said hush, Charity. You'll disturb the Visitor.'

'The who?'

Mother pointed up at the spare room over their heads. 'Ssh! He says he can't be moved until his leg's mended. He was just lucky the helicopter didn't catch fire.'

'Oh.' Charity remembered the sinister upright figure in the broken bubble. 'We're looking after the pilot?'

She said it quite casually, but the effect was extraordinary. Her mother stopped laying the tray. She stood up very straight, her face went blank and she spoke in a brisk, mechanical voice.

'It is a privilege to have the Visitor and a pleasure to look after him.'

'*What?*' said Charity.

Her mother repeated exactly the same words in exactly the same voice. 'It is a privilege to have the Visitor and a pleasure to look after him.'

A long shiver went up Charity's back, and inside her head a small voice whispered, *Something's wrong*. But what?

She turned away to open the back door. The moment the crack was wide enough, Alice was through, butting her curly head against Charity's legs and baaing with pleasure.

Above their heads, the brass handbell rang loudly. Charity's mother looked nervously upwards and then picked up the neatly laid coffee tray.

'I'll take that,' Charity said, but her mother didn't even hear her. She carried the tray upstairs herself and a few seconds later

Charity heard the low mutter of voices above.

'I don't like this,' she whispered to Alice. 'I don't like it *one little bit.*'

But before she could work out why, the car drove into the yard. Her father stepped out, shutting the door quietly instead of slamming it as usual, and came in carrying a bundle of leaflets.

'Hallo, Charity. Sleep Well?'

Charity nodded. 'Been into town?'

'Had to ask them to fix the wires. And I wanted to pick up a few things. Any coffee?'

Charity put the kettle on. Then, idly, she looked at the leaflets. Capital letters shouted slogans at her:

COOPER'S CATTLE CONCEN-
TRATES – IMPROVE MILK YIELD BY
150%!!!
CIVILIZED PIGS FATTEN UP IN
PIG-TECH PARLOURS.
TURN YOUR CHICKENS INTO EGG
MACHINES!!!
THE GOAT PRODUCTION LINE –
FROM UDDER TO CHEESE IN ONE
BUILDING!!!

At first she thought it was a joke. But she read a page or two and looked up, horrified. 'Dad! Why have you got these?'

Her father looked out the window at the untidy, tumbledown farmyard. 'We're very inefficient. We'd make more money if the farm was – well, more like a factory.'

'But you've always said you'd *never* do anything like that!' Charity shouted, and Alice baaed as if she agreed.

Her father looked vague. 'Yes, I have, haven't I.'

Charity shivered again. '*He's* made you do it, hasn't he? The Visitor.'

Horrifyingly, her father's face went blank, as her mother's had done and the same mechanical words came out of his mouth. 'It is a privilege to have the Visitor and a pleasure to look after him!'

'No!' whispered Charity. '*No!*'

At that moment, her mother came down the stairs. Pointing a finger at Alice, she chanted, 'Animals are insanitary and should be kept outside.'

It was the last straw. Grabbing Alice, Charity bolted for the only safe place she knew.

The top field, where Tom was lifting potatoes.

Alice was really too big to carry and Charity was out of breath when she got there, but Tom waited patiently while she panted everything out.

' – it's all horrible,' she finished. 'I don't know what's happening, but – if you'd *heard* them and seen those *foul* leaflets!'

Tom took off his cap and scratched his head. Then he stood up. 'Reckon I'd best go up and have a word with Farmer. Here.' He tossed the keys of the tractor. 'Make yourself useful while I'm gone.'

Charity had been driving the tractor since she was nine, but she couldn't bear to turn on the engine or do anything else except stare at the track, waiting for Tom to come back.

When he did, she hardly recognized him. He was slumped over, dragging his feet and hanging his head. Charity jumped up and ran to him.

'What's the matter?'

'A week's notice,' he said softly.

'*What?*'

'I'm too old, he says. I've to leave next week – get out of the cottage and all.' Tom looked up at Charity. 'I wouldn't want to stay, anyway. Not on the sort of farm he's planning.'

'It's that Visitor,' Charity said bitterly. 'He's changed them somehow. As if he's – as if he's *hypnotized* them.'

She looked anxiously at Tom, in case he turned mechanical too, but he just frowned in his usual slow way.

'He's got the eyes for hypnotizing all right. Big sharp green ones.'

Inside Charity's head, ideas suddenly began to move. Sharp green eyes . . . a helicopter . . . people talking as if they'd been hypnotized . . . everything being made efficient . . . But it wasn't possible!

Was it?

'We've *got* to stop him taking over, Tom.'

'How?' Tom said gloomily. 'Can't scare him off. He's no coward. Didn't even squeak when we were cutting him out of the helicopter. Just asked to borrow a pair of sunglasses. Cool as a cucumber.'

Sunglasses! Suddenly Charity had a brilliant, terrifying idea. 'Tom.' She clutched his arm. 'Have you still got *your* sunglasses? The ones your daughter sent you?'

'Those mirror specs? Maybe.'

He would have. He never threw anything away. Not even a pair of one-way sunglasses that looked like little mirrors to everyone else. Reflecting their faces back to them. Reflecting their eyes . . .

If only I dare, Charity thought as they walked down to Tom's cottage.

Half an hour later she stood outside the spare-room door with the mirror specs in her pocket, terrified. But there was no way out. She *couldn't* let Tom be sent away. With a quick knock, she pushed the door open.

As soon as she saw the tall, thin man sitting up in bed, she knew she was right. His paper-white face was stern behind Dad's sunglasses.

'Yes?' he snapped.

Charity stepped inside. 'I want to talk to you.'

The Visitor frowned. 'Idle talk is inefficient and time-wasting.'

'It's not idle. It's important. You can't take over our farm and run it how you want to It's *wrong*.'

'Your opinion is unimportant.'

'Rubbish!' Charity said fiercely. 'I'm going to stop you.'

The Visitor frowned again. 'I thought you wouldn't trouble me, but I must revise my plans.' Slowly he took off Dad's sunglasses. His eyes were extraordinary. Large, luminous. Sea-green.

Charity felt the mirror specs in her pocket. *Not yet*.

The Visitor leaned forward. 'I think you are feeling sleepy. You are *so* sleepy.' His voice was soft and crooning.

Charity's fingers curled round the specs. *Not yet*.

'So very, *very* tired and sleepy.'

Her eyelids were heavy . . . Beginning to droop . . .

Now!

She whipped the mirror specs out of her
pocket, put them on and closed her eyes.
Please let it work! It *had* to.

'So sleepy,' the voice droned on. 'Tired and
. . . sleepy . . . and . . . can't keep . . . your
eyes . . .'

Please!

'So very . . . very . . .' The voice died away
and stopped.

Charity crossed her fingers, counted to ten
and opened her eyes. The Visitor was sitting
bolt upright in bed with his eyes closed.

'Hypnotized,' whispered Charity. 'You've – '
He didn't move ' – HYPNOTIZED
YOURSELF!' She yelled. He stayed
completely still, with his eyes closed.

Taking off the mirror specs, Charity let herself quietly out of the bedroom and walked down to the kitchen.

'Mum – Dad – '

They glanced up from the plans of the new super-efficient Milking Parlour.

'It's the Visitor,' Charity said. 'I think we should call the doctor. He seems to be – unconscious.'

When the ambulance came, she was curled up on her bed making paper darts out of all the factory farm leaflets. She sent one swooping after the ambulance and then picked up *The Prime Minister's Brain* to finish reading about the Demon Headmaster. The last sentence jumped out at her.

. . . 'I wonder where he came down . . .'

Program Loop

by Jill Paton Walsh
Illustrated by Matthew Doyle

The summer he was sixteen, Robert's
parents left him alone in the house for
three weeks. His father was going to New
York on business, and his mother needed a
holiday, and wanted to go with him. Robert
had had glandular fever; think of something
for a boy to do, and he couldn't do that,
because he needed rest. He just had to stay
put and bear it. His mother stocked the
freezer lavishly, and wrote instructions on
postcards taped all over the house, before
getting on the plane, a day before his dad,
through some mix-up over tickets.

'Even convicts don't have solitary
confinement except as a punishment,' said
Robert, but only to himself. Then, on the
last day, Robert's father bought him the
computer.

'I thought it might help you to while away
an idle hour,' he said, putting the machine,
leads dangling, on the kitchen table.

Robert's eyes widened. 'That's brill, Dad!' he said. 'Mega amazing! But can we afford it?' In spite of trips to New York, Robert's father worked in a field that was all glamour and not enough cash.

'There's a lot more of it,' his father said. 'Give me a hand getting it in from the car. Where do you want it?'

There was indeed a lot more of it. A very good monitor, better than a TV set. A disc drive. A box of discs. A printer. Fanfold papers. Leads. The user manual. The disc drive was huge; 800 K.

'But can we afford this?' Robert said, as they laid it out on the desk in his father's den.

'For my boy, nothing but the best!' his father said. 'No, truth is, Robert, it's all second-hand, and I picked it up very cheap. Astonishingly cheap. As if the man wanted to sell it to me in particular. So it's all yours, and don't worry about the money.'

'Imagine having all this, and wanting to sell it!' said Robert. 'It looks new.'

'Well, I didn't actually meet the guy who used it. Bit odd, actually. He seems to have disappeared, and his father is selling up. Our good luck. Do you know how to use all this?'

'I've never had my hands on one of these before,' said Robert. 'It's very new and advanced. Supposed to be the absolute best. But I expect I can manage.'

'Good. Good. Well, I've got to pack.'

Robert spent half an hour getting all the cables plugged in and everything connected together. To connect things to the mains he needed one of those floating sockets which takes four or five plugs, and needs only one plug in the mains; there was only one power point in his father's den – the one his mother used for the vacuum cleaner. And he didn't like to buy one till he had seen his father safely off – it didn't seem friendly.

So, one way and another, it was the following day before he really settled down to work on it, and he had already experienced the long evening in front of the television set, and the amazingly dislikeable experience of going to bed without anyone to say good-night to, and going out shopping without anyone to whom to say, 'Just popping down to the shops . . .' He had every intention of getting lost to the world with his new machine.

Getting it up and running proved easy enough. It might be second-hand, but it was in perfect order. The previous owner had left not so much as a smudgy fingerprint on a key, never mind any little snags to correct. Robert summoned up the Basic he had learned at school, and began to play. First he made it print '*HALLO ROBERT YOU GENIUS*' on the screen, flashing on and off. Then he made it draw the diagram for Pythagoras' theorem. Then he started on his own project – writing a program to make it play bridge. This was really an interesting job. You had to make the machine divide fifty-two signs, one for each card in the pack, into four 'Hands' completely at random. Robert got a bug in his program, and the machine kept on making hands which repeated cards in one of the other hands. Obviously, he had to sort that out before he taught it scoring and bidding . . .

Eventually he realized he was not just hungry, but *ravenous*. It was six o'clock, almost supper-time, and he hadn't bothered with lunch. No wonder. No mum, bringing in sandwiches, or saying, 'Robert, you must eat.' Robert winced. He honestly hadn't expected to miss his mother. He had expected to be glad to see her when she got back, but actually missing her . . . Oh, well, live and learn.

But he was in a dilemma. The machine was quite warm now, having been run all

day, and Robert thought it would be better
to turn it off while he made and ate supper.
But if he turned it off he would lose the bridge
program unless he managed to 'Save to disc'
and he hadn't yet mastered the disc drive.
But he was *very* hungry. He switched the drive
on, and put one of the previous owner's discs
into it. Save 'Bridge' to disc he typed.

DISC FULL. Came up on the screen.

Robert scrabbled through the manual, and
typed *Enable. Erase.

ERASURE PROHIBITED said the
screen.

'Hell!' said Robert, and tried another disc.
The third he tried seemed to be empty, and
he stored his program safely on it, switched
off, and got himself into the kitchen. A pork
chop? No, takes time to cook, and doesn't
look too good to eat raw. He concocted a
sandwich of pilchards and peanut butter,
topped it up by eating a whole drum of rich
American ice-cream, and promptly fell asleep
on the sofa in front of the television, until the
piercing close-down tone woke him up. He
seemed to have indigestion, so he made
himself hot cocoa, using milk which had been
standing on the doorstep all day, and tasted
a bit funny. The cocoa had floaters in it, but
it was warm, anyway.

At least he had learned the value of breakfast.
The bridge program kept him going through

lunch-time day after day. He needed books,
too. He went to the computer shop to buy them.
And while he was there he noticed on a price
list for discs, the brand name, unknown to
him before, of the ten discs that had come
with the machine. Eight pounds fifty each!
More than twice the price of any others.

'Lucky you,' said the shop manager. 'Those
are the very best. They can be re-used for
ever. Just erase them, and you've got all you
need for all the programs you can write.'

Just erase them. But he kept getting the
ERASURE PROHIBITED message. He
went through the routines in the manual,
meticulously, checking every step, and still the
message came up.

Oddly, it was only after hours and hours
of struggle to erase that he thought of loading
the used discs, and seeing what was on them,
so carefully protected. *FILES LOCKED*.
ACCESS PROHIBITED, said the screen.

Robert swore. Then went downstairs to the
kitchen, and made himself a large stack of
sandwiches, and put them on a tray together
with the electric kettle, the jar of instant
coffee, and a bottle of lumpy milk, and settled
grimly with these supplies to do battle with
the devilment of the previous owner of the
machine. After some time he got a new
message on the screen. It now read *ACCESS
CODE?* The little green dot bleeped at him,

waiting. If you knew the code, you typed it
in, and then the thing let you read the disc.
The chance of guessing the code was zero.

A dis-assembler. Perhaps with a dis-
assembler he could break the code, or read it
rather, finding out the intricacies of the
program ...

He bought a dis-assembler with the last of
the holiday money his parents had left him,
and ate two large meals from the freezer.
Somehow he had gone off sandwiches. There
weren't any clean socks left in his drawer. He
put on a pair of sandals and when that left
his toes freezing he brought the electric fire
from the spare bedroom, and beamed it at
his feet. He was good at computers. Very
good. But this was a pig of a task. More
days. In desperation he read one of his
mother's postcards, ran the washing machine,
and put on clean socks, damp.

And then at last he got there. The code was

RRT841. Odd that. His own initials,
Robert Randal Thompson, and the year
– '84, and 1. Rubbish. Coincidence. All
this living alone is driving you loopy,
Robert lad, he told himself, and typed.
ACCESS CODE? said the screen.

Triumphant, Robert typed in RRT841.

On the front of the disc drive, the little red
light lit up, and the machine purred quietly.
He'd got it!

Got what, exactly?

He'd got a message that said,
*DISCONNECT VDU. CONNECT
TELEVISION.* Nothing he did would remove
this silly message, or persuade the machine to
disgorge more of whatever was on the disc.

In the end, in desperation, he did it, using
the small portable TV from the ironing room.
His mother hated ironing, and television, but
somehow found them more bearable both
together.

He set the TV down, and plugged it in.
At once the screen faded out the *CONNECT
TV* message, and said, *AT LAST. I
THOUGHT YOU'D NEVER MAKE IT.
WELL, OBVIOUSLY, I KNEW YOU
WOULD EVENTUALLY, BUT IT DID
TAKE YOU LONG ENOUGH!*

Robert looked at this message for a long
time. It made a nasty prickling sensation run
down his spine. It certainly didn't look like
any other computer message he had ever seen.

After a while it blipped off. He felt a momentary deep relief, and began to convince himself that damp socks and bad eating caused delusions in post-glandular-fever sufferers, when the screen came up with another line. *FOLLOW DIRECTIONS ON DISC.*

The chill returned. Robert thought deeply, and typed in, 'I am not who you think I am. Previous owner of machine gone away.'

The screen said *YOU ARE WHO I THINK YOU ARE. FOLLOW DIRECTIONS ON DISC.*

Robert typed in 'No.'

The screen showed *BUT I KNOW THAT YOU WILL. WHEN YOU ARE READY, TYPE 'CHAIN SHOPPING LIST'. THE DISC WILL SHOW YOU WHAT YOU ARE TO BUY.*

Robert switched everything off, and went for a walk. But the message reappeared when he switched on again. He could rid himself of it easily enough, by using the VDU instead of the TV so he could settle down to his bridge program, but of course the mysterious message nagged away at the back of his mind and eventually he gave in, and typed *'CHAIN SHOPPING LIST.'*

Purring, the disc drive showed him a list of computers. Model numbers, brand names. More or less everything on the market in the way of micro-computers. Some of the items had *BOUGHT AND SHIPPED* against them. At the foot of the list, when the machine scrolled down to it, it said, *BUY ALL ITEMS NOT MARKED 'BOUGHT AND SHIPPED.'*

Robert typed in, in a fury, 'Don't be bloody ridiculous, I can't buy all that stuff!'

WHY NOT? said the screen instantly.

'No money,' typed Robert.

OPEN A BANK ACCOUNT said the screen.

Rage shook him. He was hating this; hating being bossed about in this ridiculous way, hating himself for not being able just to switch off and ignore it. But one reason why his mother hated television was that neither Robert nor his father could ever bring themselves to switch off lousy programmes . . .

Seething, he typed in, 'I'm too young. I can't do that.'

The screen answered so fast it took his breath away: *YOU WILL FIND THAT YOU CAN.*

And of course, he did find that he could. He told the bank manager an elaborate fairy story about being alone in the house, about some bill needing paying urgently, and his father being about to put a cheque in the post, and how he, Robert, would need a paying-in book to pay it in, and a cheque-book of his own to pay the bill . . .

The bank manager was amused. 'There are easier ways of doing this, you know,' he said.

'I'm surprised at your father. But perhaps he'd like you to get used to banking early. Most people leave it till they have to handle student grants. But we like to get our customers young. Just let me know if I can help you in any way; if the letter with the cheque doesn't arrive promptly, or anything. How much money are you putting in now?'

'Now?' said Robert alarmed. 'I haven't got any till my dad sends this cheque . . .'

'Well, it isn't usual to start a bank account with absolutely nothing,' the manager said.

'I've got fifty pence,' said Robert.

'Great oaks from little acorns grow,' said the manager cheerfully.

He was quite right, too. When, three days later, Robert used his new card to request his bank balance from the automatic till, under instruction, of course, from the inexorable screen, the balance shown was £100,000.50.

It was fun, in a way, marching into computer shops buying wildly expensive things. They kept ringing the bank to check the money, and seemed very respectful when they came back. Just the same, he began to worry that all this activity might draw attention to his account, so he withdrew a huge amount in cash, remarking to the desk clerk that his father needed it to pay builders, and began to pay cash for things. He listed into the computer what he bought.

The boxes piled up in the sitting-room. And the screen talked to him. It said *ZAPPO!* when he got some prized item on the list. Sometimes he couldn't get what he wanted, the listed models were superseded, and he had to ask for further instructions. Once he couldn't get the right thing, because the code number was too high; the computer listed a Diogenes 800, and the shop said it didn't exist. There were only two Diogenes micros; 50, and 100.

EVEN BETTER said the screen. *BUY THE EARLIER MODEL.* Odd, that. Robert began to talk back a bit to the screen. 'Whoever wants all this stuff?' he asked it. 'Nobody uses all this. It isn't compatible. You choose one system and get only what goes with it.'

I AM A COLLECTOR said the screen. 'Nobody collects computers,' said Robert. *I DO* said the screen. *I HAVE LOVED THEM EVER SINCE MY FATHER BOUGHT ME ONE OF THOSE FIRST MODEL Bs WHEN I WAS A KID.*

The day came when Robert had to put a box in the hall, there being no room left in the sitting-room. He wondered what his mother would say if she saw the mess, and then he looked at the calendar, and realized it was only three days till his parents came back. He bolted up the stairs, and asked the computer how to start shipping the stuff.

THAT'S THE BEAUTY OF IT, said the screen. *IT ISN'T A PROBLEM. JUST KEEP THE STUFF.*

Keep it? Oh, gods . . .

'Impossible. Awaiting further instructions,' he typed.

AS ABOVE said the screen.

'Look, what happened to the stuff the other guy bought before he quit? Can't we do the same with all this?'

THE PREVIOUS PURCHASE AGENT GOT TOO CLEVER said the screen. *HE GOT HIMSELF SHIPPED WITH HIS LAST CONSIGNMENT. YOU CAN'T IMAGINE THE TROUBLE IT CAUSED. DON'T EVEN THINK ABOUT IT.*

'I think it's time you came clean with me,' typed Robert. 'Exactly where is all this stuff going?'

NO MARKS FOR GUESSES. NOT WHERE, WHEN. THE PREVIOUS AGENT GOT OVER-EXCITED ABOUT IT. I HAD IT ALL SET UP NICELY, A SYSTEM FOR SHIPPING ANTIQUES FROM YOUR HORIZON TO OURS AND THE IDIOT CRATED HIMSELF UP WITH A LOAD OF IBMS AND CAME TOO. THE BUREAUCRATS WERE OUTRAGED. HE JUST DISAPPEARED THEN AND ARRIVED NOW WITH NO PAPERS, NO PAST, NO CLUE HOW TO BEHAVE, NO

*MONEY . . . THEY HAVE ABSOLUTELY
FORBIDDEN FURTHER SHIPMENTS. I
WAS DISMAYED. THEN I THOUGHT
OF YOU. PERFECT. NO SHIPPING
NEEDED. YOU JUST KEEP THE
STUFF.*

'But I can't!' typed Robert. 'There isn't
anywhere!'

*ALL WORKED OUT. PUT IT
STACKED CLOSELY ON THE
BOARDED PART OF THE ROOF
SPACE, BEHIND THE COLD WATER
TANK. COVER WITH BLACK
POLYTHENE SHEETING AND
STRING. TIED DOWN AS IF ANOTHER
TANK. THEN FORGET ABOUT IT.*

'And someday I meet you? Is that it?
You're crazy. What if we move? What if I
die young? What if I won't part with the stuff
when you suddenly turn up and ask for it?'

YOUR QUESTION A said the screen.
*YOU DO NOT MOVE HOUSE. YOUR
QUESTION B. YOU DO NOT DIE
YOUNG, THAT I DO KNOW. YOUR
QUESTION C. NO PROBLEM. YOU
STILL HAVE NOT APPRECIATED
THE BEAUTY OF THIS
ARRANGEMENT.*

'I certainly haven't!' typed Robert. 'What
the hell do you mean about antiques?'

*ANTIQUE EARLY COMPUTERS IN
MINT CONDITION* said the screen.

*PURE AND PERFECT DELIGHT.
THERE WERE SO MANY KINDS IN
THE EARLY DAYS. YOU DO NOT
FOLLOW? THINK ABOUT LOOPS.*

Robert did think about loops. He thought
about them while he heaved and stacked
boxes; while he struggled with the loft ladder,
and polythene sheeting, and string; while he
lay in the bath soaking off the dirt of the roof
space, and the deathly weariness that the
heaving brought on; well, he was supposed to
be resting after glandular fever . . . he thought
about them while he chased more knowledge
through the user manual, and the dis-
assembler program . . .

His kit was networked in some crazy way.
Networked into the future computer that gave
the orders. With some ingenuity he extracted
from his disc a code for directory, and from
the directory the locking code for the user
issuing the purchase list. It was RRT20491.
Robert Randall Thompson, in two thousand
and forty nine, no doubt! Of course the
shipping would be no problem. The bossy
purchaser was himself, grown old in fiendish
ingenuity. If he kept the things, he would
own the things . . . a unique collection of
antique computers in mint condition!

But what about that figure one? What was
that doing? Robert had learned about loops.
The computer could be sent round and round
loops in the program; it could count the

number of times it went round them. One meant it was going round for the first time, but the very presence of a number meant it was going to go round more than once . . .

It mustn't. He couldn't bear it. He set his tired wits at the problem again. The computer was set for six loops. They were nested; if he touched a computer again it would find him when he was twenty-four, thirty-two, forty . . . each time the loop was shorter, one inside another . . .

He found the program line that counted the loops. Easy. This would be easy. He inserted a line. 'If n is greater than 1, END PROCEDURE' he wrote. And then, 'RUN.'

The screen cleared. He had wiped out the loop, and the program with it. The house seemed suddenly empty again, and full of relief.

He waited for his parents to come home before he investigated. Somehow their being around made him feel safer. He found he had a bank account with 50p in it. Oh, well, that would be handy when it came to student grants. There was still a pile of kit in the attic, behind the tank. He wondered if he should drag it all downstairs again sometime, and dump it in the river . . .

Then he thought, he's incredibly ancient by 2049. He's probably long past girls and drink, and any kind of fun. If the micros give the poor old geezer pleasure, where's the harm?

So he left the stuff exactly where it was.

Snake in the Grass

by Helen Cresswell

Robin could tell, right from the beginning, that he was going to enjoy the picnic. To begin with, Uncle Joe and Aunty Joy had brought him a present, a bugle.

He took a long, testing blow. The note went on and on and on – and on. He saw Auntie Joy shudder and his cousin Nigel put his hands to his ears. Nigel was twelve, and Robin hardly even came up to his shoulder.

'We'll be off now,' Uncle Joe said, climbing into his car. 'See you there.'

Robin got into the back seat of his father's car. 'It's lovely at Miller's Beck,' his mother said. 'You'll love it, Robin.'

Robin did not reply. The picnic hamper was on the back seat, too, and he was trying to squint between the wickerwork to see what was in there. In the end he gave up squinting, and sniffed. Ham, was it? Tomatoes? Oranges, definitely, and was it – could it be – strawberries?

He sat back and began to practise the bugle. He kept playing the same three notes over and over again, and watched the back of his father's neck turning a dark red.

'D'ye *have* to play that thing now?' he growled at last. 'We shall all end up in a ditch!'

'I'm only trying to learn it, Dad,' said Robin. 'I've always wanted a bugle.'

An hour later, when they had reached Miller's Beck, he had invented a tune that he really liked and had already played it about a hundred times. It was a kind of cross between 'Onward Christian Soldiers' and 'My Old Man's a Dustman'.

The minute the car stopped Robin got out and ran down to the stream. He pulled off his shoes and socks and paddled in. The water was icy cold and clear as tap water, running over stones and gravel and small boulders. Robin began to paddle downstream after a piece of floating bark he wanted for a boat, when:

'Ooooooooch!' he yelled. 'Owwwwch!'

A sharp pain ran through his foot. He balanced on one leg and lifted the hurt foot out of the water. He could see blood dripping from it.

'Ooooowh!' he yelled again 'Help!'

He began to sway round and round on his good leg, like a spinning-top winding down. He threw out his arms, yelled again and was down, flat on his bottom in the icy beck.

'Robin!' he heard his father scream. 'Robin!'

He sat where he was with the water above his waist and the hurt foot lifted above the water, still dripping blood. He couldn't even feel the foot any more. He just sat and stared at it as if it belonged to somebody else.

His father was pulling off his shoes and socks and next minute was splashing in beside him and had lifted him clear out of the water. Robin clutched him hard and water squelched between them. Robin's elbow moved sharply and he heard his father's yell.

'Hey, my glasses.'

Robin twisted his head and saw first that he was dripping blood all over his father's trousers, second that the bottoms of his father's trousers were in the water because he hadn't had time to roll them up, and third that lying at the bottom of the beck were his father's spectacles. Robin could see at a glance that they were broken – at least, one of the lenses was.

His father staggered blindly out of the water, smack into Uncle Joe who was hopping on the bank.

'Here! Take him!' he gasped.

Then Robin was in Uncle Joe's arms, dripping blood and water all over *him*, and was carried back up the slope with his mother and Aunty Joy dancing and exclaiming around them.

It was half an hour before the picnic could really begin. By then, Robin was sitting on one of the folding chairs with his foot resting on a cushion on the other chair. This meant that both his parents were sitting on the grass. Robin's foot was bandaged with his father's handkerchief and the blood had soaked right through it and had made a great stain on the yellow cushion. Robin's shorts were hanging over the car bumper where they were dripping on to Nigel's comic, Robin was wearing his swimming-trunks and had his mother's new pink cardigan draped round his shoulders. There was blood on that, too.

'*Everyone's* got a bit of blood,' he noted with satisfaction.

Admittedly, his father and Uncle Joe had come off worst. His father sat half on the rug and half off with his trousers dripping. He had to keep squinting about him and twisting his head round to see through the one remaining lens of his glasses. Robin kept staring at him, thinking how queer he looked with one small, squinting eye and one familiar large one behind the thick pebble lens. It made him look a different person – more a creature than a person, really, like something come up from under the sea.

'Are you comfy, dear?' asked his mother.

Robin nodded.

'Are you hungry?'

Robin nodded.

'Ravenous.'

'Pass Robin a sandwich, Nigel!' said Aunty Joy sharply. 'Sitting there stuffing yourself! And you'd better not have any more, till we see how many Robin wants. Bless his heart! Does he look pale to you, Myra?'

The picnic got better and better every minute. Robin had at least three times his share of strawberries and Aunty Joy made Nigel give Robin his bag of crisps because she caught him sticking out his tongue at Robin. Nigel went off in a huff and found his comic covered in blood, and the minute he tried to turn the first page it tore right across.

'That hanky's nearly soaked,' Robin said, watching Aunty Joy helping herself to the last of the strawberries. 'I've never seen so much blood. You should have seen it dripping into the water. It turned the whole stream a sort of horrible streaky red.'

Aunty Joy carried on spooning.

'If I'd been in the sea, I expect it'd have turned the whole *sea* red,' Robin went on. 'It was the thickest blood I ever saw. Sticky, thicky red blood – streams of it. Gallons. I bet it's killed all the fishes.'

Aunty Joy gulped and bravely spooned out the remaining juice.

'I won't bleed to death, will I?' he went on. 'Bleed and bleed and bleed till there isn't another drop of blood left in my whole body, and I'm dead. Just like an empty bag, I'd be.'

Aunty Joy turned pale and put down her spoon.

'Just an empty bag of skin,' repeated Robin thoughtfully. 'That's what I'll be.'

'Of course you won't, darling!' cried his mother.

'Well, this handkerchief certainly is bloody,' said Robin. 'There must've been a bucket of blood. A *bowlful* anyway!'

Aunty Joy pushed away her bowl of strawberries.

'I wonder what it could have been?' went on Robin. 'That cut me, I mean.'

'Glass!' his mother said. 'It must have been. It's disgraceful, leaving broken glass lying about like that. Someone might have been crippled for life.'

'Dad,' said Robin, after a pause. At first his father did not hear. He had stretched out at full length and was peering closely at his newspaper with his one pebble eye.

'Dad!' His father looked up. 'Dad, hadn't you better go and pick *your* glass up? From your specs, I mean? Somebody else might go and cut themselves.'

'The child's right!' his mother cried. 'Fancy the angel thinking of that! Off you go, George, and pick it up, straight away!'

Robin's father got up slowly. His trousers flapped wetly about his legs and his blood-stained shirt clung to him.

'And mind you pick up every little bit!'

she called after him. 'Don't you want those strawberries, Joy?'

She shook her head.

'Could you manage them, Robin?'

Robin could. He did. When he had finished, he licked the bowl.

Once the tea things were cleared away, everyone settled down. Aunty Joy was knitting a complicated lacy jacket that meant she had to keep counting under her breath. His mother read, Uncle Joe decided to wash his car, and his father was searching for the sports pages of his newspaper that had blown away while he was down at the beck picking up his broken spectacles. Nigel had a new model yacht and took it down to the stream. Robin watched him go. All *he* had was a bugle.

He played the bugle until the back of his father's neck was crimson again, and Aunty Joy had twice lost count of her stitches and had to go right back to the beginning of the row. For a change, he tried letting her get half-way across a row then without warning, gave a deafening blast. She jumped, the needles jerked, and half the stitches came off.

After the third time, even that didn't seem funny any more. Robin swung his legs down and tested the bad foot. Surprisingly, it hardly hurt at all. He stood right up and took a few steps. His mother looked up.

'Robin!' she squealed. 'Darling! What are you doing?'

'It's all right, Mum,' he said. 'It doesn't hurt. It's stopped bleeding now. It looks worse than it is, the handkechief being all bloody.'

'I really think you should sit still,' she said.

Robin took no notice and went limping down to the beck. Nigel was in midstream turning his yacht. It was a beauty.

'Swap you it for my bugle,' he said, after a time.

'What?' Nigel turned to face him. 'You're crazy. Crazy little kid!'

'I'll swap,' repeated Robin.

'Well, I *won't*.' Nigel turned his back again.

Robin stayed where he was. Lying by his feet were Nigel's shoes, with the socks stuffed inside them. Gently, using the big toe of his bandaged foot, he edged them off the bank and into the water. They lay there, the shoes filled and the socks began to balloon and sway. Fascinated, Robin watched. At last the socks, with a final graceful swirl, drifted free of the shoes and began to float downstream. Robin watched them out of sight. After that, there seemed nothing to do. What *could* you do, with your foot all bandaged up? The picnic was going all to pieces.

He felt a little sting on his good leg and looked down in time to see a gnat making off. He swatted hard at it, and with a sudden inspiration clapped a hand to his leg, fell to his knees and let out a blood-curdling howl.

'Robin!' He heard his mother scream. 'Robin!'

They were thundering down the slope towards him now, all of them, even Uncle Joe, wash-leather in hand.

'Darling! What is it?'

'Snake!' gasped Robin, squeezing his leg tight with his fingers.

'Where?' cried Aunty Joy. He pointed up stream, towards the long grass. He noticed that her wool was wound round her waist and her knitting trailed behind her, both needles missing.

'Where did it *bite* you?' she cried.

Robin took his hands away from his leg. Where he had clutched it, the skin was red and in the middle of the crimson patch was the tiny prick made by the gnat.

'Oooooh!' he heard his mother give an odd, sighing moan and looked up in time to see that she was falling. His father leaped forward and caught her just in time and they both fell to the ground together.

'Biting the dust,' thought Robin, watching them.

'Here!' cried Aunty Joy. 'We'll have to suck the poison out!'

She dropped to her knees beside him, her hair awry and face flushed. Next minute she had her mouth to Robin's leg and was sucking it, with fierce, noisy sucks. He tried to jerk his leg away but she had it in an iron grip. At last she stopped sucking and turning her head aside spat fiercely right into the stream. It was almost worth having her suck, to see her spit.

'Carry him up to the car!' she gasped, scrambling up. 'I must see to Myra!'

Uncle Joe picked him up for the second time that day and carried him away. Over his shoulder Robin could see the others bending over his mother, trying to lift her. Best of all, he could see Nigel beating round in the long grass with a stick while his boat, forgotten, sailed slowly off downstream.

'Gone,' Robin thought. 'Gone for ever.'

Uncle Joe put him down in the driving seat of his own car.

'Be all right for a minute, old chap?' he asked. Robin nodded.

'Have a mint.' He fished one from his pocket.

'Back in a minute. Better go and see if I can find that brute of a snake. Don't want Nigel bitten.'

Then he was gone. Robin stared through the windscreen towards the excited huddle on the bank. It seemed to him that everyone was having a good time except himself. There he sat, quite alone, scratching absently at the gnat bite.

Idly he looked about the inside of the car. Usually he wasn't allowed in. It was Uncle Joe's pride and joy. The dashboard glittered with knobs and dials. He twiddle one or two of them, and got the radio working, then a green light on, then a red, then the

windscreen wipers working. He pulled the
gear stick smoothly into neutral. To his left,
between the bucket seats, was the handbrake.
He knew how to release it – his father had
shown him.

The brake was tightly on, and it was a
struggle. He was red in the face and panting
by the time he sat upright again. The car
was rolling forward, very gently, down the
grassy slope, then gathering speed as it
approached the beck.

By the time they saw him it was too late.
The car lurched then bounced off the bank
and into the water. It stopped, right in midstream.

Robin looked out and saw himself
surrounded by water.

'The captain goes down with his ship!' he
thought.

He saw his mother sit up, stare, then fall
straight back again. He saw the others, wet,
blood-stained and horror-struck, advancing
towards him.

With a sigh he let his hands fall from the
wheel. It was the end of the picnic, he could
see that. He wound down the window and
put out a hand to wave. Instead, it met glass
and warm flesh. He heard a splash and a
tinkle. Level with the window, he saw his
father's face. Now *both* his eyes were small
and squinting. Small, squinting and murderous.

The picnic was definitely over.

Vera Pratt and the Tale of the Cow

by **Brough Girling**
Illustrated by Tony Blundell

'**W**HAT ON EARTH . . . ' said Wally Pratt entering the kitchen, 'is that?!'

'Don't be a wally Wally – it's obvious what it is, it's an off-road scrambling motor bike,' replied his mother. She wiped her forehead with an oily rag and patted the saddle of the vicious looking machine with pride. 'It's only taken me a week to build. It's got long-reach hydraulic front forks and overhead cams; it'll be just the job for next Saturday. Look.'

She pointed to a headline in the evening paper:

GRAND CROSS-COUNTRY MOTOR BIKE SCRAMBLE – FIRST PRIZE £500

'Now then Wally, don't just stand there like a blancmange with a headache, help me dry

up these carburettors and things, then you
can go out and play with your ghastly little
friends.'

'I don't know, kids today,' thought Vera,
'when I was his age I could change the big
ends on a lorry before breakfast . . . '

While Vera Pratt was thinking these thoughts
Captain Smoothy-Smythe, down at the ABC
Garage was having a meeting with his men.
In case you haven't met them before they are
his chief partner-in-crime, Dud Cheque, and
his mechanics, Slimey and Grimey, the
O'Reilly brothers.

'Right chaps,' said the Captain. 'There's
five hundred quid to be won at this cross-
country scramble on Saturday and I intend
to win it. Let me test you. Who do you think
our main opposition will be?'

'Mrs Pratt, Guv,' said Dud Cheque. 'She
always is.'

'Correct, Cheque,' snapped the Captain.
'Thank heavens you are not quite as thick as
you look.'

'Ta very much, Guv,' said Dud, pleased
with himself.

'So, what are we going to do about it?'
asked the Captain, eyeing each man in turn.

'Should we nobble her, sir?' suggested
Grimey O'Reilly.

'Nobble her? OF COURSE WE'LL
BLINKING NOBBLE HER!!' roared the

Captain. 'She will need to meet with an
unfortunate accident that will put the old girl
out of action for a long time, a very long
time. Look at this map.'

The Captain took out a large map and
spread it on his desk. 'My military experience
in the war taught me the need for thorough
planning. I've studied the course of the race,
and I believe that the best point for the strategic
unsaddling of Mrs Blasted Pratt will be here,
very near the end, where this narrow dirt
track goes through this gateway.' He pointed
to a spot on the map. 'That's Dungy Dell, on
the edge of Old Codger's Wood, near where
Shady keeps his cattle,' said Grimey O'Reilly.

'Correct. Now then,' continued the Captain firmly. 'You Slimey, will be my race mechanic, and will come to the pits with me. You Cheque, with Grimey, will be in charge of Mrs Pratt's unfortunate accident at the gate. You will achieve it with the help of this . . .'

The Captain reached down behind him and lifted a huge box on to the desk top. On the side of it were printed the words:

DAISY MOO COW –
GENUINE PANTOMIME COW
COSTUME,
complete with realistic udder
and swivelling eyes.

'What the heck are we going to do with that, Guv? said Dud Cheque, wiping his nose on the sleeve of his jacket in amazement.

'Listen carefully, and I'll tell you, idiots!' said the Captain, and he lowered his voice so that only the three of them could hear his fiendish plan . . .

Saturday dawned bright and clear.

'Where shall we watch the race from?' Wally Pratt asked his friends Bean Pole, Ginger Tom and Bill Stickers, as they trudged through Old Codger's Wood, just after lunch.

'Let's go down near the track here, it's really muddy,' suggested Bean Pole.

'OK,' said Wally, 'Mum says that the

gateway down at Dungy Dell is a really important point on the course because it's a straight run to the finish from there. She reckons that the first bike through the gate will win the race.'

'Come on then,' said Ginger Tom. 'It's just over here on the edge of the wood.

When they got there the boys agreed that it was a good vantage point. The track ran from left to right in front of them, narrow and very muddy. They sat down beside some bushes on the edge of the wood. In the far distance they could already hear the roar of revving bike engines.

'I reckon they'll be here in about five minutes,' said Wally.

'I bet your mum'll be in the lead – she's brilliant on a motor bike,' said Bill Stickers with admiration in his voice.

Suddenly the boys realized they were not alone. There were voices behind them in the wood.

'Hey,' said Bean Pole looking round, 'It's those creeps from the garage.'

'Get down!' hissed Wally Pratt through clenched teeth.

They got down and listened in amazement to the following short conversation:

'Come on Grimey, help me get the head on.'

'All right. Just my luck to be the bum.'

Moments later a very baggy brown and white cow waddled out of the wood unsteadily and stationed herself slap bang across the dirt track gateway.

'Don't forget . . .' said a muffled voice from inside the head.

'. . . the moment she falls off we've got to move forward and into the fields to let the Captain through.'

'OK, but I can't see a blooming thing in here,' said a second muffled voice from the animal's bottom.

As well as these voices the boys could hear

the sounds of approaching motor bikes. They looked at one another.

'Come on lads!' whispered Wally Pratt. 'Time for action.'

Ginger Tom and Bill Stickers ran to the cow. They very carefully lifted its plastic hoofs to reveal two pairs of men's shoes. Without the wearer's knowledge or consent they swiftly tied each pair of laces together.

'We'll need a ramp!' said Wally, and he picked up a plank from a piece of broken fence near the gate.

'Quick Bean Pole,' – he almost shouted this because of the approaching roar of a single motor bike – 'I'll get down, put this plank on top of me!'

Wally lay on his back in the mud in the middle of the track, right in front of the large cow. It was brave of him to do it, but it was for his own dear mother's sake. Bean Pole rested one end of the plank on Wally's very adequate stomach, the other he put in the middle of the track to form a steep ramp.

A split second later the mud-splattered figure of Mrs Vera Pratt, ace mechanic, her teeth gritted and her eyes fixed in exhilarated concentration on the job in hand, roared round the bend and into view.

She saw the cow.

She saw the ramp.

She did what 007 or Indiana Jones would have done. She opened the throttle of her

mighty bike to its fullest extent and she hit
the ramp as hard and as fast as she could.
She sailed across the top of the cow with her
front wheel raised high in the air.

As soon as she was safely on land again
she punched the air with one hand to
acknowledge her own impending victory, and
sped out of view.

Into view from the other direction came a
second bike. On it was Captain Smoothy-
Smythe.

Wally – his human ramp act completed –
rolled into the wood, and he and his three
friends sat spellbound as they watched the
next part of the drama unfold.

The cow's legs gave a little wiggle, but the
animal didn't seem able to move.

'Someone's tied my legs together . . . ' said
a muffled voice.

'And mine,' said another.

'OH NO!!!!!' said both voices together.

Another voice split the afternoon air.
'MOVE OUT OF THE WAY! YOU
BELLY BUM-BOILS!!' The Captain
pulled on his brakes with all his might.

But with the speed he was going, and the
slipperyness of the track, it was far too late.

He and his bike hit Daisy Moo Cow
amidships with the force of a charging rhino.

The effect was immediate and drastic. The
cow came clean in half in the middle. The
front portion fell forward on its nose, the back

fell back on its bottom. The front of the Captain's bike stopped; but the back didn't! It sailed into the air and deposited its rider face-down in the deep mud on the far side of the gateway.

The Captain lay there for a while, thinking – though it must have been very difficult to concentrate with thirty or so cross-country motor bike enthusiasts riding all over his spine.

Mr Shady Wood the local farmer was thinking too. He had been watching the race from his tractor on the far side of a field opposite Dungy Dell. He was pretty sure that he'd seen one of the motor cyclists do considerable damage to one of his brown and white cows . . .

Shady went off and had a word with Ivor Truncheon the local policeman, and as a result of this on the Monday morning following the race Captain Smoothy-Smythe was spoken to rather severely by Colonel Thundering-Blunderer, the local magistrate: 'I find you guilty of vandalism and of wilfully destroying a cow that didn't belong to you. Lager louts like you need to be taught a lesson. I order you to pay a fine. Five hundred pounds!'

Vera Pratt on the other hand spent the morning giving her son Wally a crisp ten pound note, and depositing a further £490 in her Post Office account!

The Tin Telephone

by **Nicholas Fisk**
Illustrated by Garry Kennard

Ben was upstairs, leaning out of the
bedroom window (where it was warm and
dry). Mags was right down at the bottom of
the garden (where it was cold and drizzly).

Ben was eleven and always getting new crazes. Mags was nine and always got roped in somehow.

The latest craze was the tin telephone.

Ben made it. It was simple. He took two empty tins, punched small holes in the bottom of each, then passed string through the holes. Each end of the string – there was a good ten metres of it – ended in a knot inside the tins. So when he held his tin, and Mags walked down the garden holding hers, the string was stretched tight.

All you had to do then was shout into your tin and the taut string would carry the vibrations of your voice to the other tin. No electricity needed, Nothing but vibrations.

Simple. Can't fail.

'Hallo,' Mags said into her tin.

'What?' said Ben, up in the bedroom.

'I said Hallo. Hallo, *Hallo*, HALLO!'

'Look it's no good shouting, I'm hearing *you*, not the telephone.'

'Well, *you're* shouting.'

'What? I can't hear you. Hang on. *Testing, testing, testing*. Did you hear that?'

'What?'

And so it went on, with Ben getting angrier and hotter and Mags getting damper and crosser.

'Oh, you're hopeless!' Ben said at last. He yanked the string so hard that Mags's tin telephone was pulled out of her hand. Ben shouted, 'Look, you don't seem to understand.'

'Don't want to understand!' Mags shouted back. 'You can keep your crummy old telephone!'

She stamped up the garden, thumped up the stairs and slammed the door of her room. 'Him and his stupid tin toy,' she said to herself, 'they both make me sick!'

All the same, lying in bed that night, she admitted to herself that she was sorry the telephone did not work. What fun she could have if it *did*! Her best friend Sandra was just down the road, and her other best friend Sally lived in the house opposite. If only the telephone worked, they could talk to each other for hours!

But it didn't work, so that was that.

Next day Ben had to go to school and Mags
had a half-holiday. She stayed at home.

She walked into the garden. Her tin
telephone lay under a rose-bush, where it had
fallen. She held the tin in one hand and jerked
the string with the other. The tin made a faint
boink-boink noise, a telephoney sort of noise.

'At least I can try to get some sense out of
it,' she told herself. She tied the free end of
the string to a rusty eyelet in the wall at the
end of the garden.

About this wall: it was high, slightly wavy
and saggy and made of very old, red bricks.
It was probably the oldest structure left in
the village. It had been left standing because
it would have been too expensive to knock
down; and anyhow, it was useful. It was a
fine wall, and somehow a friendly one. When
she was very young, Mags leaned her
forehead against the wise old bricks and told
the wall her troubles. Even nowadays (it was
stupid, of course) she liked to be close to the
wall – to touch it, lean against it, even rest
her cheek against its roughness. To excuse
her silliness, she reasoned that it must have
heard and felt all sorts of things. Perhaps
those things had soaked in . . .

She walked backwards from the wall until
the string was taut. Then, feeling silly, she
spoke into her tin, using a very ladylike voice.

'Hallo,' she said. 'Hall – ooo.'

Nothing happened, yet somehow she felt as if something ought to happen. The tin seemed to vibrate and thrum. It was like holding a bumble-bee.

'Hall-ooo?' Mags said.

Again, that buzzy feeling.

And then –

And then there came a tiny, tinny voice, from very far away, speaking inside the tin! 'Hallo, hallo,' it said. 'Wall speaking.'

Unable to believe what she heard and felt, Mags gasped 'Hallo? Is there . . . somebody there?'

'I'm here,' answered the voice.

Then it asked an amazing question. 'Are you a dog?' it said.

'A dog? said Mags. 'No of course I'm not! I'm Mags! A girl!'

'Oh, a girl dog,' said the voice. 'A young bitch. But you call yourself Mags? Is it a pet name?'

Mags was so flabbergasted by all this that she let the string go slack and the telephone was therefore silent. She stared dumbly at the tin. 'A dog!' she muttered. 'Why should it think me a dog?'

The tin gave her the answer. Its label showed a smiling dog with its pink tongue hanging out. And the name on the label was LASSIE.

'Aaah!' said Mags still standing with the

tin in her hand and the slack string trailing at her feet. But now she was thinking hard.

'Aaah,' she said, when she had finished thinking. This could be interesting.

She started searching for empty tins. She found them in plastic rubbish sacks. She punched a small hole in the bottom of one of them, fixed the string and ran to the wall. She tied the free end of string to the eyelet. 'Hallo . . . ?' she said.

Once again the string thrummed, the tin tingled and an answer came. But it was a strange reply. It sounded something like 'Probee eshker glasnostikoff, gadenska.'

'Pardon?' said Mags. 'I don't quite understand.'

There was a buzzy silence, then the tin said 'Oh, it's you. The girl who isn't a dog. Your name is Cherry, I take it?'

'No, I told you. I'm called Mags.'

'No, Cherry. And why aren't you speaking Polish?' the little voice demanded. 'You *are* Polish aren't you?'

Mags did not answer. Instead, she turned the tin round and round in her hand, reading the label. It read, CHERRIES IN SYRUP. So that explained the name Cherry. And underneath, in very small letters, were the words: Produce of Poland.

'Well?' said the voice in the tin. 'Say something. Speak up.'

'I'll be back soon,' Mags mumbled. She

ran back to the house to get another tin.
The new tin had contained peach segments.
She rigged it to the wall and said 'Hallo! I'm
here again!'

'Good-day, sport!' squeaked the tin, 'Good
on yer! Still a little girl are you? Got a name?
Joylene, Charlene?'

'It's still Mags,' Mags said to her tin. She
felt shy. She wasn't used to speaking to
Australians.

The peach segments came from Australia,
of course.

She went to her friends' houses asking for
tins. They thought she was mad, but gave
her their empties.

Mags tried them all,
one after another. They
spoke to her in every
language you can

think of – Israeli, Canadian, French, Hungarian, Greek, Afrikaans.

One tin even spoke to her in Russian, but not very distinctly as it was a small tin that had contained fishy stuff. The bigger tins worked best. Mags could hear really distinctly through them. They said: 'Have a nice day, you hear me?' (American); Comment ça va, ma petite?' (French); and 'Sure, and it's a soft day', (Southern Irish).

A New Zealand tin wanted to know the Test score and a Greek tin insisted on singing a long, sad, wavy song with hiccups in it.

Mags enjoyed all this, but her mind had already moved ahead. She wanted, and could not find, a very special sort of tin, a tin with a particular sign printed on it: a symbol with a lion on one side and a unicorn on the other.

At last she found the right tin. It was a beauty – big, wide and deep – the perfect sort of tin for telephoning. It still smelled of black treacle, which was nice. Best of all, it had the magic sign printed on it; also, the magic words – BY APPOINTMENT TO HER MAJESTY THE QUEEN.

Her fingers shook as she pierced the tin and strung it to the wall. Her voice shook when she spoke into it. 'Please,' she said. 'I wish to speak to Her Majesty the Queen.'

The wall, thanks to its great age and experience, got this call straight through to the Royal Apartments. A man's voice – a familiar voice – replied.

'Well, I'm awfully sorry,' it said, 'but I'm afraid you can't. The wife's out, she's exercising the dogs. I didn't quite catch your name . . . ?'

'This is Mags,' Mags replied, so breathlessly that her voice was indistinct.

'Mags?' said the man's voice uncertainly. 'Oh – *Margaret*! Haven't heard from you for ages. Your voice sounds a bit off, have you got a cold or something? Ah . . . hold on . . . you're in luck, she has just returned. I think I can put you through . . .'

In the background, Mags could hear the barking of dogs; and the sound of a lady's voice telling the dogs to be quiet and Not Jump Up On One.

And then the lady's voice came from the tin telephone, sounding very close and clear!

'What a marvellous surprise!' it said. 'It's been ages! Where are you now? Can you come here? I can't believe it's really you!'

Mags began to explain that it wasn't 'really her' at all, it was only Mags of 17 Caldicott Road – but by now the lady at the other end was shouting at the dogs telling them to behave themselves and be quiet. So Mags's explanation was not heard.

The lady's voice came once again from Mags's telephone. 'I've got a marvellous idea!' it said, 'Would you believe – there's just *nothing* in the diary between four and five-thirty! So we can have tea together! Do say you can come!'

Mags turned cold with fear. 'Please, I must tell you,' she began. But it was useless: the dogs were behaving worse than ever. Obviously their paws were muddy and they would not stop Jumping Up On One.

'Four on the dot, then!' said the lady's voice from the phone. 'We'll have a whole hour and a half together!'

The string broke and the telephone went dead. Mags was left in a daze.

What would *you* have done in her position? Would you just hide yourself away and try to forget the whole thing? Or would you scrub your nails to the bone – shine your shoes – put on your best dress – and madly brush your hair?

And then, would you rob your own money-box for the train fare, leaving enough for a taxi so as to arrive at the Palace in style . . . Is that what you would do?

Well, that is exactly what Mags did. And somehow – the wise old wall must have arranged it – the sentries let her through the great gates without any fuss at all. They even presented arms. Then a gentleman was shaking her hand and saying, 'How do you do,' smilingly; and telling her, jokingly, that there was quite a long walk ahead of her.

Then he led her through endless corridors with pictures and statues and furniture with curly gold bits.

And then Mags had tea with the Lady. What went on during that tea? What did they talk about? How did the Lady behave when she found that Mags was the wrong Mags? Regrettably, the full story can never be released. There is a thing called Protocol, and other things like Sovereignty, Royal Prerogative, Accreditation, Authorization and the Divine Right of Queens. Things like that. All that can be revealed is this: a girl was seen leaving the Palace at 5.32 p.m. precisely. She was smiling broadly. She paused at the great gates to wave at someone. And a smiling someone waved back.

If you want to know more, try telephoning Mags. A suitable telephone may be constructed from empty tins and lengths of string. This equipment is best attached to an old, mellow, experienced and friendly wall.

Finding such a wall may not be easy, but doubtless you will manage somehow.

Henry Hangs On

by Ann Pilling

Henry Hooper was short of cash. His
mother was 'between jobs' again and that
meant no pocket-money. Henry didn't
normally bother, she always paid up in the
end and he sometimes got an extra bonus for
waiting. But he needed more than a bonus
for his current project. There was a big craze
on fish tanks at school and Henry wanted
one too. Fancy fish cost money.

'I can't understand why you want fish at
all,' his mum said gloomily, staring at the
telephone. She'd gone after a job at the
Regal Cinema and she'd been waiting for it
to ring all morning. 'I think they're boring. I
mean look at next door's.'

'There's fish and fish,' Henry told her. He'd
no intention of copying Graham Snell in his
new shiny house on the other side of the
fence. Mrs Snell was mad keen on cleaning
and she thought two goldfish in a bowl were
ideal pets. No noise, no mess, no smell. And

you could get a really nice polish on the bowl
with a feather duster. The Hoopers' grotty
old house didn't get cleaned very often, and
that boy Henry went in for horrible things
like gerbils and white rats. Mrs Snell didn't
trust him at all.

'I want a tank like Nev's,' Henry said
firmly, shaking his life savings out of an old
syrup tin (97p and two rusty tap washers).
Nev was Henry's best friend. 'He's got a purple
fighting fish and a red-tailed shark, and a lot
of little stripey things that eat one another.
Real fin-nippers they are, they're great.'

'*Ugh*,' said his mother.

'It's only when they get bored,' Henry
explained hurriedly. 'That's what Nev told
me. And it doesn't happen much any more,
not now the tank's next to the telly.' (He
didn't want his mum to get the wrong idea
about this fish project. She'd be dead against
a tank full of cannibals.)

'Fancy a snack?' he said brightly. He'd
suddenly remembered the Great Baked Beans
Bonanza. One tin in every thousand had a
special label that said '£50' on the side. You
posted it off to the makers and they sent you the
money. Henry had been eating baked beans for
six solid weeks now. He was bored with them

'Not if it's beans,' said his mother
suspiciously, 'And while we're on the subject – '
Then the phone started ringing and Mrs
Hooper grabbed it. 'Hallo. Yes? Yes it is . . .

Who? . . . Oh, Mr Wainwright . . . Look, I
know we do . . . well, I'm very sorry but you'll
get it next week . . .'

It wasn't the Regal Cinema offering her a
job, it was the man who collected the rent.
Henry pulled on his anorak and sloped off.

The old market town was a good place for
bargains and he mooched up and down the
aisles. His favourite spot was the 'Nothing-
Over-A-Fiver' stall but there wasn't much
doing today. All he could see were dozens of
garden gnomes with red hats and fishing-rods.
The man on the till looked fed up.

'Gnomes Half Price' said a notice. 'But how
much?' said Henry. The gnomes looked pretty
fed up too, but he'd had a brainwave.

'Well how much have you got?' It was
raining hard and the Nothing-Over-A-Fiver
man wanted to go home. Besides, he and
Henry were old friends.

'97p,' was the glum reply, 'and two tap
washers.' The rain was dripping through the
canvas roof now, on to the little red hats.

'Go on,' the man muttered. 'Hand it over.
You can keep the washers. What do you want
the gnome for anyway?'

'Oh, you know . . .' Henry said
mysteriously, tucking it under his arm. 'It
might come in useful one of these days.'

Mrs Snell had planned an hour's weeding. In

her neat and tidy garden all the flowers stood
to attention and the grass grew to regulation
length. Even the birds sang quietly. But the
rain had driven her indoors and Henry found
her in the garage spring-cleaning the freezer.

'Want a gnome, Mrs Snell?' he said
cheerfully, coming up behind her. 'It's a real
bargain, never been used. You can have it
for three pounds.' (It wouldn't buy a fish tank
but it was a start.)

Mrs Snell jumped, dropped a bumper pack
of frozen cauliflower, and glared at him. 'No,
I do *not*, Henry,' she said. 'We have a
perfectly good gnome of our own. Where
have you got it from anyway?'

'I bought it. But I've decided it won't look
right in our garden, so I thought – '

'Well you thought *wrong*.' Mrs Snell
sprayed the freezer top with 'Sparkling
Bright' and rubbed at it ferociously with a
duster. 'A *used* gnome,' she muttered. 'The
very idea . . .'

'But it's *new*,' Henry argued (he didn't give
up easily), 'and you could – '

'No *THANK YOU*, Henry,' Mrs Snell
said belligerently. 'Now I really must get on,
if you don't mind.'

'You could always walk Kipper for your
gran,' Mrs Hooper suggested at tea-time.
(The gnome was sitting on the kitchen table,
dangling his fishing-rod into a bottle of

Daddy's Sauce.) 'She'll give you 50p if you do that.' Kipper was Gran's dog. Henry had christened him that because he had a funny smell. '50p's no good, Mum,' he grumbled. 'I need 50 *pounds* for this tank. Anyway, that dog's a fitness freak. It walks your legs off.'

Mrs Hooper shrugged. 'Please yourself. There's one bit of good news anyway. I got the job at the Regal. We might have a bit of money next week.'

'How much?' asked Henry.

'Not a lot. It's a job though. Oh, and they gave me all that stuff about "forthcoming attractions". You never know, the manager might let you in cheap now I'm on the payroll.'

Some hopes, Henry was thinking as he climbed the stairs to his attic bedroom. Mr Grout at the Regal didn't like him at all. He thought scruffy young boys like Henry Hooper lowered the tone of his cinema.

He dumped a pile of leaflets on his bed and glanced at them idly. Then he did a double-take. 'Great New Competition!' the top one said in wiggly blue letters, then in big fat red ones '£50 PRIZE IF YOU DON'T RUN OUT SCREAMING!' Henry snatched up the paper and read it right through. 'We will give £50,' it went on, 'to the first person who can sit through our SPECIALLY SELECTED HORROR FILM, *alone*, in the Regal Cinema, from ten

p.m. till midnight. BUT HAVE YOU GOT
THE GUTS? The money is yours if you can
remain in your seat till the end of the show.
No entrance fee and full press coverage.
Apply in person to the Regal Cinema, Jubilee
Road. *First Come, First Served.*'

Henry tore downstairs three at a time. Fifty
quid, just for sitting through some crummy
old film in an empty cinema. It wouldn't scare
him. The Regal was usually empty anyway.

'There's bound to be a catch,' Mrs Hooper
said doubtfully when she saw the leaflet. 'The
manager's not the sort to go throwing his
money away. It'll be a publicity stunt. People
don't go to the pictures much these days, not
now they've got videos.'

But Henry wasn't listening. His mind was
already full of fish tanks with five-pound notes
and man-eating goldfish swimming about in
them. This daft competition was money for
jam. He was going straight down to give his
name in.

'They'll not let you do it, Henry,' his
mother warned him as he zipped up his anorak.
'They'll say you're too young, or that you
don't qualify because I'm on the payroll.'

'Not till next week you're not.' Henry
reminded her. 'This film's being shown on
Friday 13th. That's *tomorrow.*'

'Look, I'm not dragging myself out to
collect you at midnight, just because of some
stupid gimmick.'

'You don't have to. I always have my tea
at Gran's on Friday and I can sleep there
after. She's only in the next street. Go on,
Mum, let me have a go.'

'Think you'll win do you?' she said with a
sudden grin. It was no use arguing with
Henry in this mood. He'd made his mind up.

'Yes I do. D'you know what the film is?
Look, it tells you. *JAWS PLUS* it's about
that millionaire who puts killer piranhas in
his swimming-pool. I've seen it three times
already, on Nev's video. It's a laugh a minute.'

Henry was in luck at the Regal. It wasn't
the manager at the cash desk it was Mavis, the
dumpy fat girl with red hair. She liked Henry.

'I want to go in for this,' he told her, pushing
the leaflet across the counter. 'Am I the first?'

Mavis looked a bit embarrassed. 'Yes. Yes
you are, as a matter of fact but – '

'Well, I definitely want to enter. See you
on Friday then, ten o'clock.'

'Hang on a minute,' she called after him,
as he pushed the swing doors open. 'What's
up?' said Henry, coming back.

'Er . . . you're a bit young I'm afraid.'

'It doesn't say anything about age on *this*,'
he pointed out, jabbing at the leaflet. 'It says
anyone can enter. Are you going to ring the
papers, Mavis? It says "full press coverage".'
Henry quite fancied a big photo of himself,
splashed across the front page.

'Terry Aspinall's covering it from the *Examiner.*'

'*Terry Aspinall?*' Henry was disappointed. He was a pimply junior reporter who'd only just left school. He did news stories like chippan fires and brownie pantomimes. 'What about the *Guardian*?' he said hopefully. 'Or the *Independent*?'

'Mr Grout left me full instructions,' Mavis told him, looking very pink and flustered. Then the door banged behind her. 'Oh, that'll be him now. Why don't you have a word with him?'

'No thanks,' Henry said hurriedly, 'Terry Aspinall will do fine. See you Friday.' And he bolted.

JAWS PLUS fourth time round was dead boring and Henry wished he'd brought a book, to pass the time. Not that he could have read it very easily. The Regal was plunged into darkness the minute the show started and Mr Grout switched on some creepy vampire music very loud. He'd been furious with Mavis for letting Henry do the competition. 'It wasn't meant for *kids*!' he shouted at her.

But Mavis stuck up for Henry. 'The leaflet says "*First Come, First Served*",' she told him, 'and Henry *was* first. Anyway, the *Examiner*'s coming to take pictures. You'll be exposed if you break your promise, Mr Grout, and

that'll be bad for business.' So there they all
were in the Regal as the hands of the clock
crept towards midnight. Bald red-faced Mr
Grout lurked at the back, willing Henry to
'run screaming' and Mavis sat at the front
dressed as an ice-cream lady willing him to
hang on. She'd heard all about the fancy fish
project, and Nev's stripey cannibals.

Henry had a slight problem, though,
staying in his seat, and as the minutes ticked
by it got more and more serious. It wasn't
the film, it was the big bottle of pop he'd
drunk at his gran's. He was starting to feel
distinctly uncomfortable, not to say bursting
but there was still a quarter of an hour to go.

'Mavis,' he whispered pointing to the green
sign that said 'Gents', '*Mavis*. I think I'll have
to slip out for a minute, it must be all the
pop I had at Gran's. Do you think – ' But
Mavis shook her head vigorously, pointed up
at the clock and then at Mr Grout. She knew
just what he was like. 'Hang on, Henry,' she
mouthed as another deadly fin flipped out of
the swimming-pool and dragged the mad
millionaire under to join his victims. 'It's very
nearly over, just *hang on*.'

So Henry tried hard, and tried to
concentrate on his fifty pounds prize. First he
crossed his legs one way, then he crossed them
the other, then he jiggled up and down in his
red velvet seat. Then he thought of the Queen
and England, and of getting a medal in

World War II. But none of it worked. It was getting worse. Quite suddenly he shot to his feet like a rocket, shoved past Mavis and disappeared into the 'Gents'. He was back in record time though, just as the millionaire's feet were being nibbled away underwater, inch by inch.

With a beam of satisfaction Mr Grout signalled to the projectionist to 'switch off'. He'd already pulled on his raincoat, and pocketed the £50 cheque. 'Sorry young man,' he said pompously, propelling him towards the exit, 'But rules are rules. Next time you go in for this sort of thing don't drink so much pop,' and he gave a nasty little smile.

'But it was a call of *nature*,' Henry protested loudly as he was bundled through the swing-doors. 'That doesn't count. It could have happened to anybody. I wasn't *scared*. And there was only a minute left.' But Mr Grout wasn't listening.

'A near miss,' he told a huddle of people waiting outside on the pavement. Terry Aspinall had snapped three photos of Henry before he could hide his red face, and there was Nev with his twin sisters, and a whole load of people from their class, all goggling at him.

'A near miss you say, sir,' said pimply Terry, licking his reporter's pencil. 'Could you explain exactly what happened?' When he heard he started to laugh. So did Nev and the twins, and all the rest of them. By

Monday morning it'd be all over their school, not to mention the paper.

Henry pulled his anorak hood right up and crept off to his gran's, leaving them all tittering outside the Regal. If only he'd not drunk that pop . . . If only he'd hung on a bit longer . . . He felt an absolute nit.

'Got your tank yet, Henry?' Graham Snell shouted across the street. 'I'm buying a lionhead goldfish next week, it's a special variety.' Henry ignored him and just carried on walking. He'd collected Kipper from Gran's and he was taking him for a good run on Darnley Moor, to forget his trouble. Trust Graham Snell to have a snobby fish.

All right so Kipper smelled a bit and tropical fish didn't. But they weren't at all friendly towards you, not like dogs, and they ate one another too. Fish had nasty habits, he'd decided; seeing *JAWS PLUS* again had put him right off getting a tank. Goldfish bowls were quite pretty, if you liked that kind of thing, but you couldn't take your goldfish for walks. Kipper was always ready to go for a walk with Henry, any old time.

Mr Browser's Nightmare

by Philip Curtis
Illustrated by Tony Ross

One day Mr Browser came home so tired after a day with Class 8 that he could hardly keep his eyes open while marking some of the sums they had done for him in the morning. Not only were Spiky and Anna and Michael their usual lively selves, but a new boy called Mop Miller had arrived. Mop claimed his dad was an inventor, and to prove it he tried to stick some of the class to the playground with a special liquid invented by his dad. What a mess!

Mr Browser went to bed early, and as often can happen to adults, he was over-tired and couldn't sleep. Many people, when they can't sleep, count sheep. Mr Browser had another method – he counted children sitting in a coach. This counting never ceased until at last he dropped off to sleep, for the children were always ducking their heads or moving

about, so that the number never came out
right.

No wonder, then, that when he did fall
asleep he began to dream about children on
a coach. The coach was outside the school,
and Mr Sage was there to see them off.

Make sure you all do exactly as Mr Browser
and Miss Causewell tell you,' he warned
them. 'All present, Mr Browser? Off you go
then.'

The driver, a fat man with bushy eyebrows,
closed the door.

'Now then,' he said fiercely. 'No eating, no
drinking, no standing up, no singing and no
making faces at drivers behind us! If you
don't behave, I won't drive!'

'What *can* we do, please?' asked Anna politely.

'Don't be cheeky,' replied the driver.

Mr Browser wasn't listening. He was looking at the new boy, Mop Miller, who was trying to squeeze a large bag on the rack above his seat.

'You've enough food in there for ten,' said Spiky Jackson.

'It's not all food,' said Mop – who was given his nickname because of his unruly fair hair. 'I've brought along one or two of my dad's favourite inventions to try out.'

'Such as?' asked Spiky.

'You wait,' replied Mop.

Mr Browser was not pleased to have overheard what had been said. He remembered the sticky liquid, and shivered. However, all went well on the journey until they neared the Tower of London. There the coach was caught in a traffic jam, and a child in a pram began to scream and pointed at the coach.

'What's going on?' demanded Mr Browser. 'Mop Miller, sit down at once!'

Mop Miller, who had been looking out of the window, turned round. Mr Browser's head jerked back from shock. Mop was wearing a horrible mask, the eyes of which were spinning round.

'Give that to me!' demanded Mr Browser. 'You've been told not to make faces at people!'

I didn't make a face,' protested Mop. 'It was the mask.'

Mr Browser put the mask on the rack, and the coach moved on.

'There's the Tower of London!' called out Emma Lee, and Mr Browser forgot about the mask while he made arrangements with the driver and saw the class off the coach. He didn't notice that Mop picked up the mask on his way out and stuffed it in his bag.

The tour of the Tower of London was going well, and Mr Browser had stopped worrying. They reached the tower in which the big executioner's axe was kept. The axe was in a transparent case and the children stared hard at it.

'My dad's invented a thing which will open a case like that,' whispered Mop to Spiky. 'It's worked by a super-conductor, which is cleverer than a micro-chip, my dad says. Bet I can run round the White Tower with the axe before anyone can catch me!'

'Don't be daft,' said Spiky. 'The axe is too heavy, for one thing.'

His eyes opened wide as Mop pulled a black box out of his bag, pressed a few buttons on it and put it on the case. The case rose up, and Mop grabbed the axe and ran off with it before Mr Browser or anyone could stop him.

'Here!' yelled a shocked Beefeater at the door. 'Bring back that axe!'

'I'll fetch it!' cried Mr Browser, and chased after Mop, who was carrying the huge axe as though it were a feather. Some Japanese tourists laughed and took photos of him. Then the bells began to ring, soldiers came running from the barracks, and all entrances to the Tower were closed.

At last Mr Browser caught up with Mop, but as he did so they were both arrested by the soldiers. The axe was returned to its place, and Mr Browser was led to the dungeons in the White Tower.

'Surely they won't behead him?' whispered Anna. They didn't, and because he was in charge of a party of children, they set him free after signing a lot of forms. Then the

party was allowed to go, watched by the
soldiers and Beefeaters.

All went well until after lunch, when they
reached Trafalgar Square.

'See Nelson's Column?' said Mop to Spiky.

'I couldn't miss it,' replied Spiky.

'Well I'm going to climb it.'

'Don't be daft!' said Spiky, but he
remembered the axe, and his mouth opened
wide as Mop took out a large pair of flippers
with very special-looking suckers on the soles.

'It's another invention of my dad's,' said
Mop. 'Just you watch me!' He swiftly pulled
the flippers over his shoes and put the mask on
his face. Then he made for the foot of the
column, and started to walk up it sideways.
Nobody noticed him until he was out of reach.

'Look at that person, Miss Causewell,' called
out Anna. 'He's climbing Nelson's Column –
and I think it's some sort of monster!'

Miss Causewell looked – and screamed.

'Mr Browser! It's Mop Miller up there,
wearing his mask.'

'Oh, no!' said Mr Browser, and then: 'Oh,
yes!'

Mop was now up as high as a house, and
walking up the side of the column as if he
were walking to school. By now a large crowd
had assembled. Policemen appeared and used
their walkie-talkies, and sirens wailed. An
ambulance and some fire-engines arrived. The

crowds were held back, and soon a helicopter circled overhead. Up and up climbed Mop, and nobody could stop him.

Nelson must have been as surprised as the pigeons when Mop reached the top and put his hand on Nelson's head. The crowd cheered and gasped when Mop started downwards again. The helicopter dropped a rope, but Mop went on walking down. As he looked downwards his mask fell off.

'It's a boy!' cried the people in the crowd. At last he was persuaded to step on a giant crane which lowered him the rest of the way.

The police took Mr Browser's name, and let Mop go, but said the cost of the fire-engines and policemen and the helicopter would have to be paid.

'I'll pay the expenses myself,' said Mr Browser, 'if you won't tell the headmaster what happened.'

The policemen shook their heads, and Mr Browser felt sick as he sat on the coach on the way home and thought about the thousands of pounds he'd have to pay, all because Mop's dad was an inventor! At least, he thought, the worst was over.

But it wasn't. Some of the class drank so much fruit juice that a stop had to be made at a small park. The children disappeared to the washrooms, and the teachers and the driver waited for them.

'They've been gone a long time,' said Miss Causewell, and then Emma Lee came running back.

'Please Mr Browser, they've all gone off on another coach on the other side of the park. The driver said it had TV on it.'

Mr Browser and Miss Causewell ran to try and catch them, but all they saw was the back of the coach disappearing down the road.

'Driver, we must catch that coach!' said Mr Browser, returning.

'Not on your life,' replied the driver. 'I'm due back at the garage at six o'clock, and I'm going home now!'

Nothing could stop him, and so the coach arrived back at the school with only two teachers and one child as passengers. A crowd of parents – and the headmaster – were waiting for the children.

'Where are they all?' cried the parents when they saw the empty coach.

'Gone on another coach,' said Miss Causewell, and fainted in the arms of the headmaster.

'Where are they? What happened?' came the cries, and they began to beat Mr Browser with newspapers and shopping bags.

'Stop hitting me!' cried Mr Browser. 'It's not my fault!'

'Wake up, dear,' said his wife, who had been shaking his shoulder. 'You must have been dreaming. Nobody's hitting you!'

Mr Browser awoke, and next morning rushed off to school to make sure the children were all there. Yes, there they were in the playground, Mop included! He sighed with relief – until Mop came up to him with a black box in his hand.

'Please, Mr Browser, would you like to see my dad's new invention?'

'Not now, thank you,' said Mr Browser, and ran into school past the headmaster and collapsed in a chair in the Staff Room.

'You look worn out,' said Miss Causewell, 'and the day has only just begun.'

'Which is better, night or day?' asked Mr Browser – but before she could think of what to say, he hurried off to his classroom in order to find out.

The Shoemaker's Boy

by Joan Aiken
Illustrated by David Lucas

Once there was a shoemaker's son called
Jem. He lived with his parents in a small
cottage and worked hard, learning his father's
trade, making and mending all kinds of shoes.
But Jem was still young, and nothing like as
skilled as his father, when a trouble came on
the family. Jem's mother fell dreadfully ill,
and no doctor seemed able to help her. Day
after day she lay asleep, white as bread,
hardly breathing, unable to eat solid food.
Jem and his father were afraid she would die.
She never spoke, never stirred. Nothing would
arouse her.

Jem's father decided to go on a pilgrimage
to the Holy City of St James, to pray that
his wife might get better.

'If St James can't help her, nobody can,'
he said. 'You be a good boy, now Jem. Look
after her as well as you can. And try to keep
the customers satisfied.'

Jem was very anxious about this, for his

father was the best shoemaker in three
kingdoms. People came from long distances
to have him measure their feet and make
boots or shoes for them. But he swallowed,
and nodded, and waved goodbye to his
father, who stuck a cockle-shell in his cap
and walked away southwards, with a party
of pilgrims on their way to the city of St
James, which was a long way off.

Weeks went by, and months went by. Jem
did his best, making and mending shoes for
the customers. Most of them were friendly
and sympathetic, knowing that his mother
was ill. But just the same, Jem longed for his
father to come back. Money was short, he
was falling further and further behind with
his orders, for he could not work as fast as
his father, nor do as much, on his own, as
the two of them did. Half-finished pairs of
shoes lay all over the shop, which was the
front room of the cottage.

One evening Jem stepped outside for a
quick breath of fresh air, after giving his
mother her supper – milk and honey, which
was all she would ever take, and that no more
than a spoonful – when he heard some faint,
shrill, twittering voices behind him, and
turned to see three strange little children.
Were they children? They had wizened little
faces, and thin, stick-like little arms and legs,
and they came no higher than his waist. They
were dressed in green.

'What did you say?' Jem asked, looking at them in surprise, for he had never seen anything like them before. Where in the world could they have come from?

'If you please, master, we have come for the three silver keys.'

'Keys, what keys?' said Jem, very puzzled. 'I have no silver keys.'

'But, if you please, master, we were sent to ask you for them. The three silver keys. They were to be left with you. And we were to collect them.'

Jem shook his head, even more puzzled. 'Nobody said anything to me about three silver keys. You must be mistaken. And where in the name of goodness did you come from, you queer little beings?'

But when Jem said 'in the name of goodness' the three rickety little creatures disappeared – vanished clean away – phttt! – just like that!

Jem rubbed his eyes, and rubbed them again.

'I must have dreamed them,' he said to himself. 'I'm tired, that's all.'

He had good reason to be tired. For, night after night he sat up watching over his mother, feeding her a spoonful of milk every hour.

That evening he worked late, and was about to lie down on the cobbler's bench for half an hour's rest, when there came a loud knock at the door.

'Bother it! Maybe it's those three children back again,' thought Jem, not at all pleased at being disturbed. He was in no hurry to answer. But the knock came again – thump, thump! – very loud and impatient. It sounded too loud for the children. So Jem sighed, rubbed his eyes and his face, crossed the room, and unbarred the door.

Outside stood a knight. In the dusk of the evening Jem could just see that he was dressed in black – over his armour he had a black tunic, and his shield and helmet were of black metal, his cloak was black, and so was the great horse that stood behind him, steaming and stamping and shaking its head.

'Hey boy! Will you make me a pair of boots?' said the knight. 'I have heard that the ones you make here are the best in the land.'

'Oh, sir, I'm afraid my father is away from

home,' said Jem. 'I may not be able to make a pair as well as your honour wishes.'

'You look to me like a clever boy, as well as a truthful one,' said the knight. 'I will take a chance; for I have travelled a great distance to come here.'

Indeed, when the knight had walked into the shop, and Jem had lit a candle, he could guess that this must be so; the knight's cloak and tunic were worn and dusty, and the boots he wore were split and cracked.

Jem knelt to measure the knight's feet. He was too polite to say anything, but the shape of them surprised him greatly; he had never seen such feet before in his whole life. And, by now, Jem had measured a great many feet.

'What is the price for a pair of boots?' said the knight.

'One guinea, sir.'

'I will give you two guineas. But the boots must be finished by breakfast-time.'

Jem thought if he worked all night, he could just about manage this. And two guineas would buy enough milk and honey to last his mother for weeks, besides leather and firewood and candles and thread and shoemaker's needles.

'I will try to have them ready for you, sir,' said Jem, reaching for his shears to begin cutting the leather.

'The boots must be black. Oh, and by the way,' said the knight, very carelessly, as he turned to leave, 'I think three silver keys have been left here for me? You might as well give them to me now.'

Outside the door, the knight's black horse let out a shrill neigh; the sound was so loud and sudden that it brought Jem's skin out in goose-pimples.

'No, sir,' he said. 'I'm afraid you are wrong. Nobody has left any keys with me.'

'No? Perhaps they will have before I come for the boots. Keep them for me carefully.'

And the knight strode away. He did not say goodbye. And Jem felt a great deal more comfortable when he had gone, and the sound of his horse's hoofs had died away.

That night, Jem worked harder than he ever had in his life before, cutting and snipping, stitching and stretching and shaping. One candle burned clean away, and he had to light another; still, never mind, the black knight's money would pay for plenty of candles. One boot was finished, and the other well begun, when he heard another knock at the door.

'Oh, plague take whoever it is,' thought Jem. 'It can't be the black knight back yet, for it's not long past midnight, nowhere near breakfast-time. Maybe it is those green children again, botheration befall them!'

He called out, 'Please go away, whoever you are! I'm very busy.'

But a soft voice answered, 'I promise I will take no more than a moment of your time.'

Something about the voice made Jem think
of his father. It certainly did not belong to
those odd little children. So – rather
impatiently – he unbarred the door again and
looked out.

The moon was up now, and by its light
he could see a white knight standing on the
path. His cloak and tunic were white, his
armour was of silver, so were his sword and
the helmet that hung on his shoulders. On
his shield Jem could see a crest showing three
keys.

'Good evening, Jem,' he said. 'I am sorry
to disturb you at your work, but I have heard

that you are a good and trustworthy boy. I have come to ask a favour of you. You see this little packet? I need to leave it in a safe place while I go on an errand. May I leave it with you? And will you make sure that nobody touches it?'

The knight handed Jem a small square of folded white silk, about the size of a purse, tied across with dozens of threads.

'Why certainly, sir,' said Jem, puzzled but polite. 'I'll keep it carefully for you, if you wish. It shall go up here, on my top shelf. And I will see that no one touches it. But when will you be back for it?'

'If I'm not back by daybreak,' said the knight, 'you may keep the packet. Good-night to you now.' And he sprang on to his white horse, which bolted away with the speed and silence of lightning.

Jem put the packet on the shelf, relocked the door, and went back to work. Now he was very tired indeed, and found it harder and harder to set his stitches. His head nodded, and what was worse, he thought he kept hearing voices. He heard the voices of the green, shrivelled children, wailing and squeaking outside the door.

'Let us in, Jem! Let us in to sit by your fire! We are perished with cold, Jem, we are hungry and freezing. We need those three keys, we need them dreadfully – let us in please, let us in and give us the keys!'

'I have no keys for you!' Jem shouted, waking himself out of his dream, and he set to work again, harder then ever.

Then he thought he heard the black knight, riding round and round outside the cottage; and he heard the black horse stamp and snort and whinny.

'You had better give me those keys, Jem,' shouted the black knight.

'I can't do that, sir. I promised that no one should touch them.'

'Fool boy! Those keys were left there for me!'

Jem shook himself and trembled as he thought he heard the horse whinny again. And then he heard what sounded like a wild battle: there were thumps and clangs and bangs, shouts and blows and screams, the neighing of several horses and the trample of many hoofs.

'Whatever is going on out there is no business of mine,' thought Jem, 'my business is to get this boot finished.' And he ducked his head over his work, stitching and stitching away for dear life. Once or twice he went to see how his mother was, in the back room, wondering that she was not roused by the sounds outside; but no, she lay as before, in her deep strange sleep.

Just before daybreak the second boot was done. 'They are by far the best boots I have ever made,' thought Jem, looking at them with pride as they stood side by side on the bench, soft and supple, finely stitched, and gleaming with polish.

Now there came a crashing thump on the door; the bolt broke and the door swung open. There stood the black knight, looking blacker than ever against the slowly growing light of day. He was all dusty and bleeding, his armour hacked and gashed, his shield was scratched and dented, so was his helmet, through the bars of which his eyes gleamed angrily.

It was plain that he had been in a fight, and, by the look of him, had had the worst of it.

'I've come for my boots, boy,' he snapped. 'Are they ready?'

'Yes, sir, quite ready,' said Jem, and pointed to them, standing on the bench.

'And I'll have those keys, too.'

'I have no keys for you, sir.'

'Don't lie to me! The white knight left the keys for me, in a packet of silk. There they are, on the shelf. It was for me he left them!'

The knight stepped forward to snatch the packet from the shelf, but Jem was before him, whipped them away, and sprang to the back of the shop, where he stood holding the little silk square with its crisscross of thread.

'Give it to me!' hissed the knight, through the bars of his helmet. 'Take off that cursed wrapping and give it to me! Or I will slice your head clean off.'

'No, sir. I have no right to give it to you.'

The black knight moved forward a step, pulling his sword from the scabbard – and, just at that moment, the old rooster, perched on the roof above, crowed cockadoodledoo!

Jem saw the pair of black boots he had made wither and shrivel away like burned paper in a blaze; looking above the boots he saw that the black knight, too, had vanished clean away.

Nothing was left but the little white packet that he held in his hand.

'Well,' thought Jem, 'the white knight did say that, if he was not back by daybreak, I might keep the packet. And the sun has risen. So I may as well open it and see what is inside.'

Very carefully he snipped through all the threads that tied the packet, across and across. Then he undid the white silk wrapping. He had expected to find three silver keys, but no, he found only a little square of thin, soft white bread. Quite fresh it seemed, considering that it had been wrapped and tied up so tight for who knows how long.

'Jem!' came his mother's voice faintly through the door, 'Jem? I'm hungry, Jem!'

'Mother! Are you feeling better?'

Jem was thunderstruck, for it was months since his mother had spoken.

'I'm so hungry,' she said, faintly stirring. 'Oh, how I would like to eat a little piece of fresh white bread.'

*

Two months later, Jem's father came home –
thin, worn, weary, footsore, grey-haired, with
his clothes frayed and torn and tattered. But
oh, how happy he was to see his wife strong
and active and pink-cheeked again, and to
find how well his boy Jem had managed,
making and mending shoes and boots,
keeping the customers satisfied, during the
long, long months of his absence.

And when they asked him – 'Yes!' he said.
'I got to the Holy City of St James. What a
place! With a church the size of a whole
forest! And I begged the saint to help us –
and see how quickly he answered my prayer!
But there was one moment, on the way, when
I thought I should never reach the city, or
see you again. For a band of brigands, led by
a wicked fellow in black armour, set on our
party in wild mountain country, and I'm sure
they would have killed us all if we had not
been rescued, at the very last minute.'

'Who rescued you, Father?'

'A white knight, all dressed in white. He
was the best fighter I've ever seen – finished
off half a dozen of the robbers, and the rest
turned round and ran for their lives. The
knight wouldn't even stay to be thanked –
said he had another errand, a long way off,
and he galloped away before we could even
find out his name. But the crest on his shield
showed three keys . . . '

William Darling

by **Anne Fine**
Illustrated by Amy Burch

It isn't even my real name that's wrong. I can see that if I'd been *born* with a name like William Darling, if it was written in great curly letters across my birth certificate or something, then I might have to put up with it. But it isn't even my proper name!

I had trouble from my first day at school. I was in more fights than anyone Mrs Hurd could remember, and she'd been teaching for twenty years. It took weeks for some of the people in my class to realize that, when they sidled up and whispered 'Hallo, William Darling,' I was going to turn round and biff them. I don't like to hear people teasing my father.

Mind you, it's his own fault. He started it off. I'm sure he didn't mean to cause me any trouble. It just worked out that way. You see, my father's *terribly* old. His hair's all silver, he gets arthritis in damp weather, and he uses huge, spotted cotton handkerchiefs, not paper tissues, to blow his nose when he gets a cold. (He makes the most extraordinary trumpeting noise. People look round.) He had another family, all grown up before he even thought of marrying my mother and starting on me. They drop in every now and again, and it's so odd to think they're my half-brothers. They look old enough to be my father. And my father looks old enough to be my grandpa.

And he's old-fashioned, too. He likes things like starched sheets and fountain pens you fill from glass ink bottles, and mealtimes so late that Mum and I have practically starved to death before they're even on the table.

And he calls me William Darling.

He doesn't mean anything by it, I know. He doesn't *want* to make my life difficult. It's just he's too set in his ways to change.

He should have grown up at Wallisdean Primary School. He'd know a lot better then! He'd know that it's quite all right if your mother leans over the fence and calls out 'Hurry up, darling!' Nobody thinks twice about it. Nobody even seems to *hear*. But if your father does it, you're in big trouble – or a lot of fights.

Me, I was in a lot of fights. It took weeks before my father could stroll along to school with me, in the morning and hand me my lunch-box, saying, 'There you are, darling,' without great choruses of sniggers breaking

out all around me. I had to get tough with
Melissa Halestrap for eight days in a row
before she learned to stop lifting my coat off
its hook at the end of the day and handing it
to me with a really good imitation of my
father's voice: 'Come along, William Darling.
Button up. Freezy cold outside!'

No it wasn't easy. I had to work at things

at Wallisdean Primary. But I managed. And
in the end I was perfectly satisfied and happy
(and even Mrs Hurd admitted to my mum
at the jumble sale in aid of the school roof
that I'd stopped all that frightful fighting and
matured a lot.) Then, suddenly one day, the
bombshell dropped.

'And when you move on to your next
school in September . . . ' That's all Mrs
Hurd said. (What I mean is, I was so shocked
I didn't listen to the rest.) I'm not *stupid*. I
knew I was in the school's oldest class. I knew
we moved on. So I must have realized it was
our last term at Wallisdean. It's just I hadn't
realized how soon the change was. And,
worse, it suddenly struck me that, just as I'd
finally persuaded everybody in this school
that it was a really bad idea to try and get
away with calling me William Darling, I'd
have to start all over again somewhere else.

And it would be even harder than before.
Everyone would be older, and the older you
get, the sillier William Darling sounds to you.
And though I didn't know exactly what sort
of teasing you get in the new school, I felt
pretty sure of one thing: it would be worse.

I fretted about it, on and off, for the whole
of the last two weeks of the term. And
through the start of the summer holidays.
Then, when I saw that worrying was spoiling
everything, I reckoned I'd try tackling the
matter head on. I thought it would be best.

'Please,' I said to my father. 'Since I'm
starting at a new school, will you try to get
out of the habit of calling me William
Darling?' He lowered his *Financial Times* and
peered at me over it through the gold-
rimmed, half-moon spectacles he wears three
quarters of the way down his nose.

'Quite understand,' he told me. 'No
problem, sweetheart.' You can see why I
wasn't optimistic. William Sweetheart is no
better. And when, by the end of the week,
he'd called me pumpkin, poppet, lambkin
and muffin in his attempts to avoid the
dreaded word, I just gave up.

Only three weeks to go. Have to try
something else. Sulking. I'd try sulking. I
wouldn't answer him. If he called me William
Darling, I'd go all fish-faced, and refuse to
respond to it. It didn't work, of course. He
hates me being miserable. He hovered over
me the entire week.

'What's the matter? Something up? Do tell.
Oh what a gloomy bird you are, darling!'

No luck there, then. And only two weeks
to go. I was getting so desperate I thought
I'd try bribery. I've found that bribery often
works when all else fails.

'If I weed the whole garden,' I wheedled.
'Properly. Front *and* back. *And* down the side
behind the garage. *And* along the verge – '
His spoon drifted to a halt half-way between

his breakfast bowl of stewed prunes and his open mouth. One bushy silver eyebrow shot up. I thought he might be going to have a heart attack.

'If I do all that, will you stop calling me William Darling?'

'Of course I will William, darling!'

'Starting right now!'

'Yes, d–' He practically had to choke it back with the stewed prunes. 'Yes, William.' He practised it to himself sternly, several times, in between mouthfuls. 'Yes, William. Thank you, William. Oh really, William? Quite so, William. Quite so.'

I left him chuntering, and strode out determinedly to the tool shed. I worked the whole day. I never stopped, except when Mum brought out a plate of sandwiches and shared them with me on the steps, admiring all the work I'd done, and helping me replant all the marigolds I'd pulled out of the ground by mistake.

At half-past five I finished the very last square millimetre of the verge. I waved triumphantly to Mum, and she went to fetch him.

They came back arm in arm. They strolled around the garden together as if the place were owned by the National Trust, praising everything, and gasping at how tidy it looked. Then he turned round and pressed a brand new shiny ten pence piece into my hand. (He

often does this. He's so old that he thinks ten
pence is a fortune. It's one of the worst things
about marrying someone a lot older than
yourself, Mum says. You spend a fiver, and
they think you are wicked.)

'Thank you,' I said, and put the coin in
my pocket.

'Don't lose it,' he warned me.

Don't lose it! I get ten of them every week
for pocket money. He must know that. But
he's in the habit of keeping shiny coins he
comes across in a special pocket in his
waistcoat, ready to press them on the
deserving, and he's too old to bother to
change. So I held my tongue. Pity he didn't.

'Splendid!' he said, waving to indicate my
handiwork. 'You've done a beautiful job,
William, darling!'

Mum tried to save the day. She spun him
round and started pointing out how well the
sweet peas were growing up the wall. But I
was desperate. I'd slaved all day, and I'd got
nowhere. I couldn't help it. I just lost my
temper. Hurling the hoe down on the lawn, I
yelled at him that I'd spent the *whole* day
working because we'd made a deal, he'd
promised me, and what happens? What's the
very first thing he says? William Darling! I
threw my arms out, and wailed dramatically:

'What can I *do*? I'm not a baby any more!
You've got to get out of the habit of calling
me William Darling!'

It's always a bad move losing your temper in front of anyone over fifty-five. They're old enough to think it's disgraceful.

'Listen to me, William,' he said. 'Manners like that simply will not do. I am extremely sorry that, so soon after our little agreement, the word happened to slip out. But tantrums are quite inexcusable. Pick up that hoe.'

I picked up that hoe.

'And kindly apologize to your mother.'

I muttered something that might, or might not have been 'Sorry Mum'. She didn't mind. She understood perfectly well how ratty I was getting about the whole business. *She* knew I'm not a baby any more. *She* understood that things would be very different at a new school.

And maybe that's the reason she fixed up that arrangement the next day. Maybe that's why she made a special point of making my father take me into town shopping. 'He needs an awful lot of new stuff,' she said. 'You can take him.'

'Me? Why *me*?' (He hates shopping. He says the assistants are 'too big for their boots' and don't know the first thing about what they're selling. He nearly had a stroke last year when the girl in Woollies paused in the act of snipping the elastic thread Mum was buying, and asked how many centimetres there were in a metre. Mum pretends it was the girl's shocking mathematics that so upset him. But I know better. I know it was the fact that, until then, he hadn't realized yards, feet and inches had gone.)

'You have to take him,' Mum insisted. 'Because I'll be at work. And you're retired.'

No arguing with that. He had to take me.

He didn't enjoy it. First we went into Brierleys to buy an electronic calculator – not any old cheap one for beginners, but the sort my new school recommends, the Fz 753xb, which does all manner of fancy things I certainly hope I'll never need.

'Bit sophisticated, isn't it?' he said, inspecting the price sticker with even more interest than the calculator itself. 'For a child.'

The shop girl gave him a pretty cool look.

'Pretty sophisticated maths they do at this young man's age,' she retorted.

He looked around for the young man, and was a bit put out to just see me.

'Hrrrumph,' he said. But he wrote out the cheque, and signed it with his extraordinary flourish.

Then we went to Skinners to buy football boots. As soon as they found a pair that fitted me, he handed over the cheque he'd been filling out while I was lacing up.

'Eight pounds, twenty,' he said.

She shook her head and handed the cheque back to him with the neatly written bill.

'Twelve pounds, ten pence,' she corrected him. 'Your boy is in the larger foot range now.'

Without saying a word, he tore the first cheque into tiny pieces. Then, still without speaking, he wrote out another.

He was in quite a mood by the time we reached Hilliards to buy my new blazer. He strode straight over to the rack which had the smallest sizes hanging from it, and had to be steered to the taller rack behind, where all the larger (and more expensive) ones hung.

'Bit pricey,' he complained.

'Wait till he shoots up,' said the shop assistant. 'He'll grow out of a blazer a week!'

My father looked horrified. When he wrote the cheque, his hand was trembling. It can't be easy for a man who still thinks that ten pence is wealth.

He claimed that he needed some time to
recover.

'Bills, bills, bills!' he groused. 'Let's go and
have a cup of tea while feeling returns to my
cheque-signing fingers.'

He chose the same old tea-shop we've gone
to for years. (Mum says they bought their
first high-chair for me.) We took our usual
table, and my father gave the usual order to
the new summer waitress.

'One lightly buttered toasted tea-cake, and
a Balloon Special.'

(Maybe I should tell you that, with a
Balloon Special, you get three flavours of ice-
cream, and a big red balloon tied to the back
of your chair.)

The waitress gave me a suspicious look.

'He looks a bit old for a Balloon Special,'
she said. 'It's only supposed to be for sevens
and under.' (She was so new, she still
remembered the rules.)

'Really?' said my father frostily. 'Then two
lightly buttered toasted tea-cakes.' I didn't
argue. I suddenly reckoned I understood why
my mum had been so keen to send us off
together. She wanted him to realize for
himself I wasn't a baby any longer. I did
hard maths. I had big feet. If I'd grown out
of big red balloons and into tea-cakes, maybe
I'd also grown out of being called William
Darling.

I wasn't his darling right now, that was for

sure. He was flicking back through the cheque-book.

'Bills, bills, bills!' he grumbled. 'You're costing me a fortune. I ought to call you "bill"!'

The assistant sailed over with the tea-cakes.

'One for me,' said my father. 'And one for "bill" here.'

She laid the tea-cakes down without so much as a flicker of her eyebrows. She obviously thought what he said sounded perfectly normal. And so it did, of course – bill–William–Bill! I couldn't believe my luck. The joke amused him so much, he kept it up all the way home: 'Tired, bill?' and all through the evening: 'Nice mug of hot chocolate, bill?' and at bedtime: 'Cleaned your teeth, bill?' The joke ran for weeks. Sometimes I worried that he might be on the verge of finding it boring, but I'd just leave out my calculator, or my blazer, or my new football boots, and he'd be off again: 'Getting ready for school, bill?'

And, to my amazement, the joke was still making him chuckle right through the last days of my holiday, and the parent's evening. Grinning, my father introduced me to my new form teacher.

'This is my bill,' he said.

Mr Henry looked at me.

'Hallo, Bill.'

That was all he said!

And it went on that way. I couldn't believe my good fortune was holding. When I walked

in the classroom on the first morning, all Mr
Henry said was, 'Here, Bill. These books are
for you,' and by the break everybody called
me Bill as if I'd never in my life been William
Darling.

I stayed Bill all through lunch, and all
afternoon. I stayed Bill all week – no fuss, no
fights. Mrs Hurd would have been astonished.
She wouldn't have known me. I worried
sometimes, quite a lot because I knew I
couldn't keep my father away from the school
grounds for ever, but then I'd put the anxiety
out of my mind, and just enjoy things.

And then, this afternoon, it finally happened.
Our class were playing football on the pitch
when suddenly I caught sight of my father's
straw boater sailing along on the other side of
the school hedge. I kept my head down,
dreading the moment I just *knew* was coming
the instant he reached the gap at the gate,
glanced in, and saw me. Chills ran down my
spine. My knees were shaking. Did I have
time to run off the pitch?

Too late! Over the gate I heard his clear,
clear voice.

'Go for it, William, darling! Boot that ball!'
The football was sailing down towards, me
head on. Swinging my foot back, I booted it
as hard as I could, *really* hard, as if to let the
teasers know, right from the very start, what
I could do.

The ball flew down the pitch in a perfect arc.

Then I looked round. No teasers? Mr Henry called out 'Well done, Bill!' as he puffed past, but no one else was paying the slightest attention. No one was even looking my way. They'd all gone haring up the field after the ball, and I suddenly realized that no one had, even for a single moment, connected me with that silvery-haired (and probably confused) old gentleman who yelled encouragement over the fence, and then strolled on. William Darling? No. No William Darling in this game, I'm afraid. Me? Oh, my name's Bill.

The Old Woman Who Lived in a Cola Can

A modern telling of a traditional tale by

Bernard Ashley

Illustrated by Colin Hawkins

Not all that long ago, and not so far away, there was an old woman who lived in a Cola can. 'All right,' you'd hear her say, the place *is* small, definitely chilly in December and scorching hot in July – but the floor never needs a coat of polish, and there's no dark corners where a spider can lurk.' The old woman reckoned it wasn't at all a bad place for a home, especially seeing there wasn't a penny to pay in rent.

One day, though, she went in for a telly, and she suddenly saw all sorts of things she'd never seen before. She saw all the adverts and loads of films – but instead of making her happy, all the new things only made her mad. She shouted and swore and shook her fist at the programmes.

'Rotten shame! Rotten shame! T'aint fair –

it ain't fair!' she created. 'Why should I make
do in this tinny little place when there's some
lucky devils got nice flats in brand new tower
blocks, with lifts to take them up and chutes
to send the rubbish down? What's wrong with
me I'd like to know. Why can't I have a
chance to be choosy?'

She went on like that for ages, banging
and clanging inside her can – till one day, by
a stroke of luck just before her voice gave
out, someone special heard her from the road:
a flash young man who had won the pools and
was looking for ways to get rid of his money.

He couldn't get across the grass to her
quickly enough.

'Gordon Bennett, darlin', what a noise,
what a *girls and boys*! But I heard what you
was shoutin', and I've got to say I do feel
sorry. I do. I feel choked, *prodded an' poked*.
But say no more, girl an' just keep your
pecker up. Give us a couple o' days for some
wheelin' an' dealin', watch out for the motor
– an' we'll see what we're gonna see!'

So the old woman said no more. She
switched off her telly, kept her eyes glued to
the road, and before the milkman had been
round three times, the flash young man was
back, sitting on his motor and calling out
across the grass.

'Come on , love, get out of the can! Jump
in the car, the old *jam jar*, and come along o'
me. I'll soon sort you out.'

She didn't need telling twice. She jumped in his car, just as she was, and before you could say knife, there she was in the town, in a nice little flat in a brand new block, with a lift to take her up and a chute to send the rubbish down.

And she was over the moon with delight. But she clean forgot to say thank you to the flash young man. And anyway, he had shot off to get on with his spending. He'd gone to the races, and smart sunny places, to Catterick, Corfu and Crete. But after a while, when his mouth ached with smiling, he thought he'd go back to see how the old woman was getting on.

And what did he hear when he got there? The tinkle of friendly tea-cups, a few contented sighs like the summer wind in net curtains?

Not a bit of it. Just the slamming of doors and shouts enough to wake the caretaker.

'Rotten shame! Rotten shame! T'aint fair – it aint fair! I'm just about up to *here*, miles off the ground in this pokey little flat – when there's some folks in the know got houses in streets, and their own front gates, with cars out the front and patios round the back. What's wrong with *me*? I'd like to know. Why don't I get the chance to be superior?'

The flash young man listened to every word she said. He kept dead quiet till he'd heard everything: then he put his eye to the spy-hole and he shouted through the door.

'Cheer up, doll,' he pleaded, 'no need for
all that. Say no more, girl, and keep your
pecker up. Give us a couple o' days for some
wheelin' an' dealin', watch out for the motor
– an' we'll see what we're gonna see!'

So the old woman said no more. She
stopped banging doors, kept her eyes on the
parking-bays, and before the kids had ruined
the lifts three more times, the young man
was back, leaning on his bonnet and calling
up at her balcony.

'Come on, love, get down them stairs!
Jump in the motor, the old *haddock an' bloater*,
and come along o' me. I'll soon sort you out.'

She didn't need telling twice. She ran down
the stairs, jumped in the back, and before she
could say Jack Robinson, there she was in a
neat town house in a proper little street, with
car out front and a patio round the back.

She was over the moon with delight. But
she clean forgot to say thank you to the flash

young man. And, anyway, he'd shot off to
get on with his spending. He'd gone to casinos
and sporting club beanos, to Monte, Majorca
and Maine. But after a while, when his hand
hurt with winning, he thought he'd go back
to see how the old woman was getting on.

And what did he hear when he got there?
The contented creak of an old cane chair,
the sound of soft singing to Radio Two?

Not a bit of it. Just the slam of a swing-bin
being attacked and shouts which ran to the
end of the road.

'Rotten shame! Rotten shame! T'ain't fair
– it ain't fair! Here am I shunted off in this
common little house – when there's some
people live it up in tree-lined cul-de-sacs, with
nicely spoken neighbours and a man to do
the grass. What's wrong with *me*? I'd like to
know. When do I get a chance to be posh?'

The flash young man heard everything she
said, then he rang upon her chimes.

'Heaven help us, love, what a state! What
a terrible *two-an'-eight*! We can't have this.
Give us a couple of days for some wheelin'
an' dealin', watch out for the motor – an'
we'll see what we're gonna see!'

So the old woman said no more. She
stopped kicking-in the kitchen and packed her
bags instead. And before she'd carried the
dustbin through three times the flash young
man was back, elbow on the dashboard and
tooting at the door.

'Come on, love, leg it over that gate! Jump in the Bentley, the old *gently-gently*, and come along o' me. I'll soon sort you out.'

She didn't need telling twice. She slammed herself into the car with her hat in her hand, and before she could say one o'clock, there she was in a double-fronted house in a cul-de-sac, with nicely spoken neighbours and a man to do her grass.

And she was over the moon with delight. But she clean forgot to say thank you to the flash young man. And anyway, he'd shot off to get on with his spending. He bought up some pubs and three football clubs, United, Juventos and York. But after a while, when he got fed up with watching other people run around, he thought he'd go back and see how the old woman was getting on.

And what did he hear when he got there? The plop of fresh coffee being poured for the vicar, the rinsing of hands to get spoon polish off?

Not a bit of it. Just the rip of a radiator off of a wall and shouts loud enough to divert the traffic.

'Rotten shame! Rotten shame! T'ain't fair – it ain't fair. Here am I overlooked in this middle-class place, when Lords and Ladies have mansions in big country parks, and servants to send off to Harrods. What's wrong with *me*? I'd like to know. When do I get the chance to be Upper Crust?'

The flash young man caught every word she said, then made his way round the back.

'Hold your horses! Half-time!' he called through the tradesmen's entrance. 'You'll make yourself sick, *Uncle Dick*! Say no more, girl, and keep your pecker up. Give us a couple of days for some wheelin' an' dealin', watch out for the motor − an' we'll see what we're gonna see!'

So the old woman said no more. She put a few favourite bits into a suitcase − and by the time she'd turned three collecting-tins away from her door, the flash young man was back, purring into the driveway and breaking the beam on her burglar alarm.

'Come on, love, let's move it. Jump in the Jag, the old *boast an' brag*, and come along o' me. I'll soon sort you out.'

She didn't need telling twice. She shot in as fast as the speed of greased lightning, and before she could say hell for leather there she was in a mansion, a duchess no less, with servants to send off to Harrods and a tiara to put on her head.

And she was over the moon with delight. But she clean forgot to say thank you to the flash young man. And, anyway, he'd shot off to get on with his spending. He bought up an airway to make a cheap fare-way for tourists on trips to the States. But after a while, when he got fed up with being pointed at, he thought he'd go back and see how the old woman was getting on.

And what did he hear when he got there? The click of a croquet ball sent through a hoop, the flow of a pool being filled?

Not a bit of it. Just the sound of a summer-house being destroyed, and shouts loud enough for three counties to hear.

'Rotten shame! Rotten shame! T'ain't fair – it ain't fair. Here I am just a two-bob old duchess down here, when there's SOMEONE WE KNOW with a crown on her head! What's wrong with *me*? I'd like to know. When do I get the chance to be Royal?'

The flash young man took note of what the old woman said, then he made an appointment to see her.

'Your Grace, what a row! What a *bull and a cow*! You are comin' on strong. But I know what you mean, so you don't need to say another word. Give us a couple o' days for some wheelin' and dealin', watch out for the motor – and we'll see what we're gonna see!'

So the old woman said no more. She threw her tiara into the pool, kept her eyes peeled for the car with no number, and before she had time to sack three of her maids, the flash young man was back, gliding up towards her in his silver Rolls-Royce.

'Come on, ma'am,' he invited. 'Jump into the Roller, the *top hat an' bowler*, and come along o' me. I'll soon sort you out.'

She didn't need telling twice. She got into the back, cocked her head on one side, and started waving away out of this window and that. And before she could say, 'It gives me great pleasure,' she was there.

Back in her home in the Cola can: where, yell as she liked, she lived for the rest of her life.

But she never saved up for a telly again – and she wouldn't have said thank you if you'd given her one.

Acknowledgements

The Publishers gratefully acknowledge the following, for permission to reproduce copyright material in this anthology:

The Shoemaker's Boy text copyright © Joan Aiken 1986, illustrations copyright © David Lucas 1986; *The Old Woman Who Lived in the Cola Can* text copyright © Bernard Ashley 1984, illustrations copyright © Colin Hawkins 1984; *Crash Landing* text copyright © Gillian Cross 1987, illustrations copyright © Bob Harvey 1987; *Snake in the Grass* text copyright © Helen Cresswell 1986; *Mr Browser's Nightmare* text copyright © Philip Curtis 1988, illustrations copyright © Tony Ross 1988; *The Fancy Dress Party* text copyright © Marjorie Darke 1985; *William Darling* text copyright © Anne Fine 1990, illustrations copyright © Amy Burch 1990; *The Tin Telephone* text copyright © Nicholas Fisk 1989, illustrations copyright © Garry Kennard 1989; *Vera Pratt and the Tale of the Cow* text copyright © Brough Girling 1990, illustrations copyright © Tony Blundell 1990; *Shark and Chips* text copyright © K. M. Peyton 1991, reprinted by permission of the author, illustrations copyright © Tony Blundell 1991; *Henry Hangs On* text copyright © Ann Pilling 1987; *Program Loop* text copyright © Jill Paton Walsh 1986, illustrations copyright © Matthew Doyle 1986; *Super Gran's Pedal Power* text copyright © Forrest Wilson 1988, illustrations copyright © David McKee 1988.